# *Micromegas*
## *and Other Stories*

## Voltaire

Translated by Douglas Parmée

Foreword by Nicholas Cronk

ALMA CLASSICS

ALMA CLASSICS LTD
London House
243-253 Lower Mortlake Road
Richmond
Surrey TW9 2LL
United Kingdom
www.almaclassics.com

*Micromegas* first published in 1752
This edition first published by Alma Classics Ltd in 2014

Translation and Introduction © Douglas Parmée, 2014

Foreword © Nicholas Cronk, 2014

Cover image: Øivind Hovland

Printed and bound by CPI Group (UK) Ltd, Croydon, CR0 4YY

ISBN: 978-1-84749-379-8

# Contents

# Foreword

## Voltaire and Tale-telling

When Jeannot (in 'Jeannot and Colin') is down on his luck, he
seeks advice from a nobleman:

> "Why not write novels?" asked a witty courtier. "In Paris that's
> a very handy way of making money."

Voltaire was not, clearly, a fan of contemporary fiction. He had
made his name as an author with a Virgilian epic about Henri IV
and a verse classical tragedy, *Oedipus*, which triumphed at the
Comédie Française in 1718, when he was still only twenty-four
years old. In taking as his models Virgil and Sophocles, the ambitious young writer set out to shine in the literary genres of classical
antiquity, and his early reputation was founded on his brilliance as
a poet, not as a writer of prose. When he did come to write prose
later on, after his stay in England in the 1720s, he wrote mainly
works of history and polemic. But his range was remarkable, and

he attempted virtually every known literary genre – to be precise, every known literary genre except one: he detested the novel. The "novel" in Voltaire's day meant the meandering adventure stories of a Prévost or, worse, the wordy sentimental novels of a Richardson, and these Voltaire deplored for being long and boring. After struggling through *Clarissa*, he remarked sourly that "I wouldn't like to be condemned to have to read it again".

Voltaire's own taste in prose ran to works that were more incisive and more ideologically engaged – like the tales in this collection. The genre of the "short story", as we understand it in the Anglo-American tradition, would become established in France in the course of the nineteenth century, with such writers as Nodier, Mérimée and, above all, Maupassant. But short fiction was enormously popular in France in the eighteenth century, and thousands of works of widely differing types were published, all loosely clustered under the umbrella title of *conte*, or tale. The great attraction of the tale was its loose and unregulated structure, which left authors free to invent and experiment. There were children's tales of course, fairy tales aplenty, and the French reading public took a particular fancy to the tales of the Arabian Nights, brilliantly recreated in French by Antoine Galland. Parodies of the oriental tale were a particular favourite, promising easy eroticism, while other authors, like Marmontel, wrote tales with heavy-handed moral lessons ('Jeannot and Colin' both imitates and parodies the *conte moral*). The term *conte* was so woolly that it even embraced tales told in verse – Voltaire wrote those too.

Literary genres like classical tragedy or epic were prestigious but rule-bound; the *conte*, on the other hand, precisely because it was modest and seemingly unimportant, was open to experimentation of all kinds. Voltaire's tales are often referred to collectively as *contes philosophiques*, "philosophical tales", and critics like to argue that Voltaire found in fiction an effective way of conveying certain of his philosophical preoccupations, such as the question of evil that is central to the plots of 'Memnon' and of 'The Way of the World'. According to this idea, the fictional whimsy of the tale provides a sugar-coating to help the reader swallow the pill of some otherwise unpalatable truth. But do these tales deliver up clear truths? Or even suggest any solution to the problems they raise? Readers must decide for themselves what to make of the book of truth at the end of 'Micromegas' whose pages turn out to be blank. As the narrator says in the closing words of the 'Story of a Good Brahmin',

> So how can this contradiction be resolved? This isn't a matter to be lightly dismissed: it still requires a great deal of discussion.

Voltaire himself never used the term *conte philosophique*, a label which seems to have been invented in the late nineteenth century as a convenience for teachers in the classroom – the nearest Voltaire ever comes is with 'Micromegas', which he subtitles 'A Philosophical Story' (in French, *Histoire philosophique*): and *histoire* (meaning both "story" and "history") means something very different from *conte*.

Surprisingly, Voltaire never published his tales in a single collected volume (which is typically how we read them nowadays). For Voltaire, each *conte*, however brief, could stand alone. 'Micromegas' was just long enough to constitute separate publication as a brochure, and in the case of the shorter tales, Voltaire liked to publish them alongside works that were completely different, creating effects of contrast (and surprise): 'Memnon' and 'The Way of the World', for example, were both included in a miscellany, the *Collection of Works in Verse and Prose*, which appeared in 1749; then, over twenty years later, 'Memnon' unexpectedly reappeared in a philosophical dictionary, the *Questions on the Encyclopedia*, as the article 'Confidence in Oneself' – these tales are nothing if not flexible. The two tales 'A Short Digression' and 'An Adventure in India' first appeared as part of *The Ignorant Philosopher* (1766), a book about sceptical thinking, and the stories were evidently included to underpin and complement the broader philosophical aims of the work. Voltaire's tales are different in nature, therefore, from nineteenth-century short stories, which were normally published in story collections.

Another way in which the eighteenth-century *conte* differs from the more "literary" nineteenth-century short story is in its emphasis on the spoken nature of storytelling: the French noun *conte* recalls the verb *conter*, "to tell a story", so the notion of orality is inherent in the name of the genre. Dialogue plays a large part in many of these tales (indeed Voltaire composed numerous dialogues which closely resemble the *contes*), and characters within the stories will often narrate a tale, as when Memnon encounters a lady in distress:

> She told him her tale, full of emotion… Memnon was taking her story greatly to heart and feeling all the time a growing desire to help such an honest and unhappy young woman…

– a warning, if one were needed, of the dangers of responding to tales too naively.

In Voltaire's *contes* we are typically made conscious of the narrating voice, and the "I" is often present from the very beginning: "In the course of my travels I met an old Brahmin…" begins the 'Story of a Good Brahmin'; and 'Scarmentado's Travels' are, as the subtitle announces, "written by himself": "I was born in 1600 in Candia… I remember a mediocre poet called Iro…" Similarly, the narrator in *Cosi-Sancta* takes us by the hand as he leads us through the story, remarking at one point, "since, as I've already pointed out…": the sense of oral delivery is always to the fore in these tales. The "I" who narrates is not Voltaire himself, of course, yet the easy and familiar form of address creates a sense of intimacy with the tale-teller. The story 'Wives, Submit Yourselves unto Your Own Husbands' introduces a new twist, when the hitherto discreet narrator suddenly surprises us with a casual aside: "One day when the Abbé de Châteauneuf, my godfather, called on her…" The Abbé de Châteauneuf, a society man of letters who had died in 1703, was indeed Voltaire's godfather, and this seemingly gratuitous detail is dropped in to prod us into thinking that perhaps the narrator really is Voltaire after all...

Other writers of the period have fun with the spoken conventions of tale-telling – we think of Diderot's tale 'This Is Not a *Conte*', which plays games with the self-reflexive nature of fiction. Voltaire's aim is different, however, as he draws our attention to the intrinsic orality of the *conte* in order to discredit the very form in which he is writing. This comes as something of a shock, but Voltaire's brilliant narrative verve should not blind us to the fact that he tells tales in order to subvert tale-telling. To understand this irony and appreciate Voltaire's deep-seated mistrust of the oral tradition, we need to look to his view of history.

It had long been held that educated men should study the history of the ancient world, because it was there that one found the best examples of proper moral conduct. Against this view, Voltaire argued strenuously that it was the study of *modern* history that mattered: its lessons were more pertinent to modern concerns and the existence of recent printed sources meant that modern history was more reliable. Significantly, modern history began, in Voltaire's view, with the Renaissance and the invention of printing. Earlier history, he felt, was based on little more than storytelling, and in his all-encompassing condemnation of (as he saw them) primitive societies, he lumped together as equivalent the worlds of Homer and the Bible, each as fanciful as the other. For a man trained by the Jesuits to argue rationally on the basis of the firm evidence of printed sources, the "oral tradition" was anathema: it implied a reliance on doubtful manuscripts dating from a time before the age of printing, synonymous with superstition and unreason. Voltaire was an intensely bookish individual, never happier than when sitting in a well-stocked library, and the idea of an oral culture ran counter to all his principles as a man of the Enlightenment.

Faced by an ancient historical or theological text, Voltaire's greatest term of abuse is to brand it a "fable": as a character in 'Jeannot and Colin' remarks, "all ancient history only consists of hackneyed fables". In 'An Adventure in India', there is a hilarious description of Bacchus "walking across the Red Sea without wetting his feet", these details, the narrator notes, "faithfully recorded in the Orphic oracles": for Voltaire to imply an equivalence between Bacchus and Moses is daring enough; but to hint that biblical Scriptures might be as fanciful as mythological accounts is seriously provocative. The Romantics would bask in nostalgia for the oral traditions of lost societies – think of Ossian – but nothing could be further from Voltaire's urban and urbane way of thinking. In becoming a teller of tales, Voltaire sets out to parody and undermine the assumptions of the "primitive" oral tradition underlying earlier historical accounts – including the Bible. These seemingly modest tales rank among Voltaire's most provocative works.

A picture by the Genevan artist Jean Huber depicts Voltaire waving his arms about as he tells a story to a group of seated peasants: the image, often reproduced, is charming, and seems somehow to tame Voltaire's tale-telling. It is easy to read the tales as elegant and witty examples of his art, but we should not be deceived. Voltaire was a radical writer who sought deliberately to challenge and provoke, and his *contes* are all the more hard-hitting for being so seemingly innocent. Voltaire's tales are essentially about the lunacy of man's unreason, or, as the opening line of 'Memnon' memorably puts it, "the odd idea of being perfectly wise". And, as the newspapers remind us on a daily basis, there is no more dangerous subject than that.

– Nicholas Cronk
Director of the Voltaire Foundation,
University of Oxford

# Introduction

Voltaire has often been acclaimed as a universal genius. This seems a doubtful claim – he is no Goethe – but that he was a popularizer of genius is clear. He was certainly an innovative political and social historian, amongst the first to base his findings on documentary sources rather than anecdote or chronicle – some of this slips into his *contes*, particularly 'Scarmentado's Travels'. He wrote prolifically: a few comedies; a great number of tragedies (about fifty overall), many successful in France and elsewhere; two epics, both of which led him into trouble: in *La Pucelle*, he had the impertinence to include burlesque elements in the sacred story of Joan of Arc; numerous philosophical essays and many articles for the *Encyclopédie*, the clarion call of the French eighteenth-century Enlightenment, although he himself had considerable reservations on the power of reason and complete distrust of metaphysics; countless odes, epistles, verse satires, a libretto for Rameau and other ballets; some rather amateurish works on science – he was an early French convert to Newton, whose works he learnt about largely from Newton's friend and pupil, Samuel Clarke; several influential studies on politics; a multitude of subversive dialogues and pamphlets, largely attacks on organized religion and religious fanaticism – in which paradoxically he himself became, at times, fanatical. He was a passionate polemicist, especially in later life, in the cause of justice, and an indefatigable correspondent – over 15,000 letters have survived.

Today, of this splendid output, admired and celebrated in his day, little remains: history now demands fuller research and documentation; odes, epistles and suchlike are outdated genres; verse tragedy has survived only when written by a genius, as has lyrical and epic poetry – nobody has ever claimed to find such genius in Voltaire, nor does anyone read epics other than those of the greatest: Homer, Virgil, Dante. Science marches on and so does philosophy: nobody would now read Voltaire for scientific or philosophical enlightenment. A lot of his ideas were second-hand: there is an amusing anecdote told by the eighteenth-century moralist Chamfort. D'Alembert, a great mathematician and, with Diderot, co-editor of the earlier volumes of the *Encyclopédie*, is talking to a distinguished Swiss jurist, who comments that, while he admired the universality of Voltaire's genius, there did seem to be gaps in his knowledge of civil law. "Yes," d'Alembert replies, "and I found him a little weak only in his grasp of geometry." In a word, Voltaire's knowledge and even many of his ideas in general are largely borrowed.

In one genre, however, borrowed knowledge is no handicap and, added to wide personal observation, humour and wit, can lead to fame: the *conte*, in which Voltaire triumphantly survives.

Mention his name in any gathering of people still fond of reading and someone, or even more than one, is likely to say: "Yes, indeed – *Candide*." *Zadig* may also be mentioned, even one or two other titles. Voltaire is still alive and kicking, indeed a genius, in his tales. They contain everything associated with the adjective Voltairean: irony, satire, levity, irreverence towards icons, questioning of established authority and taboos, notably in religion; universal and unending problems of ignorance, intolerance, stupidity – you name them – Voltaire has them in his sights.

This selection of tales is a mixed bag, something for all tastes; it lays no claim to being exhaustive but it does cover certain areas not found in *Candide* or *Zadig* and since these *contes* are shorter, they offer more concentrated entertainment. They follow the chronological order of their composition, as far as this could be ascertained with any degree of accuracy.

'Cosi-Sancta' can be traced back to around 1714, when Voltaire was frequenting the salon of the Duchesse du Maine, who organized amusing evenings or *nuits blanches* – sleepless nights – when, instead of going to bed, guests would draw a letter out of a bag and improvise a story. N meant a novella and, on this particular occasion, the person who had drawn it didn't feel competent; Voltaire impulsively offered to undertake the task – the result of which was 'Cosi-Sancta'. It bears the marks of haste and inexperience, a somewhat crudely simple story largely concerned with adultery, a common subject in French short stories and one in which the duchess and her circle would have expert knowledge.

There is a touch of irony but little wit. The subtitle will, however, be of interest to the reader: it is pure Machiavelli – the end justifies the means – and foreshadows Voltaire's later tales of political philosophy. It has a whiff of casuistry which he might well have picked up from his teachers at Louis-le-Grand, as well as a hint of Voltaire's interest in religious questions, which eventually came to obsess him and make him a zealous propagandist against fanaticism rather than a mere jesting philosopher.

'Plato's Dream' (1736 or 37), is very different and far subtler. Voltaire was over forty years old, raring to go, able to invent amusing and imaginative plots and already in a crafty, mischievous mood. He proposes the odd hypothesis that the Demiurge, the Great Creator of the Universe, has delegated some of its creation to underlings, on the unlikely pretext of testing their competence. Among these fanciful ideas, Voltaire also provides some quite false information about Plato's alleged assertions – the *conte* genre allows such liberties, and Voltaire took them without compunction. For example, despite Voltaire's flight of fancy Plato did not maintain that there could never be more than five perfect worlds. Voltaire is attributing various silly and pointless assertions to an acclaimed philosopher, presumably to warn – and perhaps even to mislead – his reader: he is advocating universal scepticism. In 'Plato's Dream', the final tease is uncomfortably unexpected – and comic.

'Micromegas', composed largely in the late 1730s, and published only in 1752, takes us straight into *Gulliver's Travels* territory, to meet a sort of Brobdingnagian. It includes space travel (already exploited in the previous century by Cyrano de Bergerac's account of a journey to the moon). It also foreshadows science fiction, the use of very odd microscopes and hearing aids. It examines various political themes and slyly mentions one of Voltaire's adversaries Pierre Louis Maupertuis. The main message of 'Micromegas' is clearly that, however gifted the human race may be, it is too presumptuous, too clever by half and more stupid than it imagines. We see him particularly scornful of the followers of Nicolas Malebranche, who believed in constant divine intervention.

'The Way of the World' (1748) follows a line already traced by Montesquieu in his *Lettres persanes*; instead of bringing Persians to Paris, Voltaire takes the unsophisticated Scythian Babouc to Persepolis, aka Paris, easily recognizable to contemporaries by obvious references to abuses of the time – the sale of regiments, the *fermiers-généraux* who bought the right to collect extortionate taxes, the low status of actresses, the ponderousness of the legal system, etc. In a word, we see the splendours and miseries of man and, since we're in Paris, particularly of woman. We also find a brief consideration of the stupidity of war, which always inspired disgust in Voltaire, though, true to form, he treats the subject with ironical amusement. In any case, not even a philosopher should be expected to practise what he preaches, particularly when he does it with a smile. Babouc weighs up all the evidence, and one Parisian female, of course, Teona – thought to have represented Mme du Châtelet – almost tempts him to stay. But duty calls, he goes home and makes his somewhat ambiguous report, too complicated to express in words; Ituriel gets the message.

'Memnon', composed at about the same time as 'The Way of the World', is less hopeful but great fun – at least at the beginning. A man decides to follow the tenets of Epicurus: i.e. strictly limit his desires, steer clear of women, eat and drink in moderation, live within his means, stick with a few good friends. So simple – and naturally, it all goes wrong. How does Voltaire succeed in making such a sad story untragic? Partly because such a sudden and swift stream of disasters is absurdly implausible and Memnon is depicted as such a silly idiot that the reader is led to think that he's lucky to have got off so lightly. Looking more closely, we realize that Voltaire has achieved a deeper understanding of the nature of the *conte*: while the situations may or may not be plausible, we are not seeing real people but marionettes on a string being jigged about, very rapidly, by a highly skilled puppeteer: the characters have length and breadth but little depth, so that we're amused rather than moved by their antics. In 'Memnon' this feeling of distance, of aloofness, is enhanced by the introduction of a supernatural celestial being. Nonetheless, Voltaire has still, in these rapid sketches – swiftly flowing narrative is another of his great skills – while entertaining us, managed to add a pinch of wisdom.

The 'Letter from a Turk' again takes us briefly back to the Orient; the author has extra scope for fantasy. But one significantly serious aspect of the *conte* is plain: we are shown a Muslim and a Brahmin joined in friendship, despite their different faiths. The fun comes from the fakirs who, we note, when offended, can quickly be appeased with a small tip; money talks here, as it will in 'Scarmentado's Travels'.

'Scarmentado's Travels' is an earlier, more pessimistic version of *Candide*, a work showing a young man on a journey of apprenticeship to life; it also shows Voltaire as a historian: the date of Scarmentado's birth fits the time when the events he recounts, give or take a few years, did occur. Written shortly after his ignominious retreat from Prussia, the wounds are still festering: the title is derived from the Spanish *escarmentar*, meaning "to give someone an unpleasant lesson", and Voltaire has just received one. The tone throughout is devastatingly ironic, not least because of the cheerful, nonchalant, dispassionate tone in which the protagonist relates the most appalling events. Here and there we do find the Voltairean lighter touch, as when, to further his education, Scarmentado visits Rome: he meets a paedophile theologian (still a topical subject today) and he just manages to escape unscathed; he also meets a couple of priests (vowed to chastity) and succeeds in frustrating their unchaste lust for a young woman; but Rome does have its charms, though they're not human... After this, in country after country, we see horror upon horror. The only relatively civilized country he visits seems to be China, for which Voltaire always had a soft spot: China had a purely secular official religion, Confucianism, and all other religions were tolerated, as long as they did not threaten political stability; to live civilized lives, men need only to behave decently towards each other. But

Scarmentado's stay in China is short, and after unpleasant experiences in India and Africa, with amusing details (a large part of the Voltairean charm lies in humorous asides), he is glad to get back safely home to Crete, happily married (though his wife has certain weaknesses – again the Voltairean touch).

'Consolation for Two' shows partial recovery of Voltaire's spirits. Although sadness and tragedy may still be round the corner – here we are reminded of 'Memnon' – we are amused at Citophile's futile attempts to cure the unhappy reality with bookish citations – he is the prototypical, insistent, self-important, albeit well-meaning bore familiar to all gatherings, every club, every board meeting. Such cures must be left to nature, in which Voltaire had great faith – far greater than in doctors. Only time is the great healer – a trite moral, like most of his morals, enlivened by the amusing tale leading up to it.

'The Story of a Good Brahmin' again takes us eastwards, though not into exotic fancy. We're given a brief but penetrating insight into Voltaire's preoccupations: on the surface, a mere illustration of Pope's "Where ignorance is bliss, 'tis folly to be wise", it turns into a more confidential, personal and even anxious examination of the value of knowledge and wisdom. However, as so often (too often?), Voltaire is happy to leave his reader on a humorous, ambiguous note: he hands the problem back to his reader.

Readers of 'Jeannot and Colin' slowly become aware that they are in unusual territory: this is a moralizing rather than a philosophical *conte*. The account of the rise and fall of the ambitious

Jeannot Senior is obviously a criticism of greed and that of Jeannot Junior's social career a satire on vanity. However, Voltaire's wit once more succeeds in enlivening the conventional morality: the solemn family conference held to determine what studies a young man needs to undertake to make his mark in smart society is vintage Voltaire.

The mobility of his mind and his unbounded curiosity come once again into full flower in 'Wives, Submit Yourselves unto Your Own Husbands', published shortly after 'Jeannot and Colin'. We meet an unexpected Voltaire – an amusing feminist or quasi-feminist. Madame de Grancey may not be faultless: she is promiscuous, self-willed and vain – she could be a man… But she knows her rights and expresses them forcefully, and she is better read and more cultivated than her military husband. She has very definite views on religion. Voltaire also manages, through the voice of his godfather, Châteauneuf, to correct some of her misconceptions about Islam. It's a rollicking pot-pourri, but with subtle asides. Mme de Grancey's wish for a book on the rights of women would be granted only in the early 1790s by Mary Wollstonecraft's book with that very title.

The 'Short Digression' dates from 1766. Age has by no means dulled the old man's verve: it is again a pungent reminder to mankind of its ignorance, its inability to think deeply or even straight; men thus have to be told what to think by a dictator, a clever dictator who is happy to change his position when he realizes he's gone too far – the perfect politician, of any period. And there's a sting in the tail.

In the 'Adventure in India', written during the same period, we are back in the East, a world of fancy and yet all too real. Rather oddly, we meet, very briefly, yet another potential Voltaire – a vegetarian! But we're soon in the familiar world of nature in the raw, seldom mild, and witnessing man's inhumanity to man: a world of cruelty, ignorance and injustice. It was in the year of its publication that the nineteen-year-old La Barre was unjustly executed. What can one do in such a world? It's every man for himself!

The final tale is 'The Adventure of Memory'; we have moved on ten years to 1775 and Voltaire had only three years left to live. He still feels that Lockean empiricism needs emphasizing to the Sorbonne (for which he creates the anagram *Nonsobre*) and to the prominent religious factions of Jesuits and Jansenists. Deprived of our memory to store our sense impressions, we lose our common sense. This tale in particular reminds us of Voltaire's permanent distrust of metaphysics of any sort. It's very diverting and all too short: Voltaire has succeeded in making us smile at a reconstruction of what we now know as Alzheimer's, a disease which is, in fact, appallingly tragic. Incidentally, the *philosophe* with dangerously empirical views about cheese is thought to have been Helvétius, whose ideas greatly influenced Bentham and other utilitarians.

Why have Voltaire's *contes* alone survived and promise to continue to thrive? Two lines of Pope suggest an answer:

> True wit is nature to advantage dressed,
> What oft was thought but ne'er so well expressed.

The basic requirement is knowledge of human nature, and Voltaire would lay no claim to originality for being so well aware of its shortcomings: cruelty, intolerance, selfishness and so on – the list is endless and it makes us uneasy. It is here that Voltaire takes charge: these failings are and always will be with us and, being universal, are of permanent concern. But he knows ways to alleviate their impact: one is to accumulate the number of disasters to the point of absurdity; another is to hurry us through them so fast that we haven't time to be too shocked or grieved. And to this shrewd understanding of human nature, he adds his special genius: the gift of a superb raconteur, of introducing sly comments, wry hints, casual unexpected irrelevancies, an anticlimax, an ambiguity that will bemuse and amuse us; he's using the recipe of digressions – in the words of Sterne, "incontestably the sunshine, the life and soul of reading". His wit, and especially his humour, will make us smile – not laugh, for Voltaire life is no laughing matter; our tensions will have been relaxed, the charm has worked. He might, indeed, otherwise be considered unfeeling, lacking enthusiasm, too negative, but we must remind ourselves that he is not writing moral tales, and 'Jeannot and Colin' warns us that he was not cut out to be a sentimental moralizer. Should any readers wish for a more emotional, more positive attitude, Jean-Jacques Rousseau is at their service; one doesn't exclude the other. Indeed, during the French Revolution, Voltaire's early influence was replaced by adulation of Jean-Jacques. But it is certainly more fun to listen to Voltaire, that smooth old fox, chatting away – this is the Age of Conversation – wittily and with tongue in cheek, even about mishaps and disasters. In the words of another sly and witty rogue, Beaumarchais (who impoverished himself by organizing an early collective edition of Voltaire's work): "We must make haste to laugh, for fear of having to weep."

– Douglas Parmée

# Micromegas
### and Other Stories

# Cosi-Sancta

## A Small Sin to Achieve a Greater Good

### AN AFRICAN TALE

THERE'S AN ERRONEOUS MAXIM saying that it's wrong to commit a minor evil in order to achieve a major good. St Augustine himself agrees that this maxim is untrue, as we can see from his account, in his *City of God*, of this little adventure which happened in his diocese during the proconsulate of Septimus Acidynus.

There was an old priest in Hippo who was very fond of setting up fraternities and hearing confessions from all the girls in his parish; he had the reputation of being inspired by God, because he also indulged in fortune-telling, a pastime which he was rather good at.

One day they brought a young girl called Cosi-Sancta to see him: she was the most beautiful person in the province. Her parents were Jansenists and had brought her up according to the strictest moral principles; not one of her suitors had ever for a moment entered her thoughts while she was praying. A few days earlier, she'd been promised in marriage to a wizened old man by the

3

name of Capito, a councillor in the presidium of Hippo. He was a surly, moody little fellow, no fool, but his conversation tended to be stiff, and he had a tendency to mock and wasn't averse to playing nasty tricks on other people; what's more, he was as jealous as a Venetian and could never have been on friendly terms with any man who showed a liking for his wife. The poor young creature was doing her utmost to love him, as he was destined to become her husband, but however hard she tried she was having no success.

She was coming to consult the old priest to find out if hers would be a happy marriage. In a prophetic tone of voice, the good man pronounced: "My daughter, your virtue will cause many misfortunes, but one day you will be made a saint, because you will have been three times unfaithful to your husband."

The beautiful, innocent girl was astounded and deeply troubled on hearing this oracle. She burst into tears and asked for an explanation, thinking that these words might contain some mystical significance, but the only further explanation the old priest would give was that "three times" meant being unfaithful with three different men, not on three occasions with the same man.

Cosi-Sancta screamed and even said rude things to the old priest, swearing that she would never become a saint. But, as you're about to learn, she was wrong.

The marriage took place shortly afterwards: it was a very grand wedding and she managed to listen quite patiently to the poor speeches that she was forced to hear, the well-worn innuendoes, the scarcely veiled indecencies which are traditionally included to embarrass a modest young bride. She danced very gracefully with a number of very well-built and pleasant young men who didn't look in the least pleasant to her husband.

With some reluctance, she got into little Capito's bed, spent most of the night asleep and woke up still dreaming, not so much about her husband but about a young man called Ribaldos who somehow or other had crept into her thoughts. This young man seemed to have been shaped by the hand of Love, of whom he had the charm and boldness and roguish ways. He behaved somewhat indiscreetly, but only towards those women who invited such behaviour. He was the darling of Hippo, arousing ill feeling between all the women of that city and among all their husbands and mothers. He usually chose women as the fancy took him, and partly to satisfy his vanity. Cosi-Sancta, however, he truly loved, and he loved her all the more because she was hard to get.

First of all, like any intelligent man, he began by ingratiating himself with the husband, taking every opportunity of talking to him, telling him how well he looked, laughing at his jokes, admiring his polished manners, losing when playing cards with him and continually confiding in him. Cosi-Sancta found him extremely amiable and though she didn't suspect that she was already fonder of him than she realized, Capito did and while being as conceited as any little man may be, he didn't fail to detect that the purpose of Ribaldos's frequent visits was far from being for his sake only. He trumped up a pretext to break off relations with the young man and forbade him to come to the house.

Cosi-Sancta was very vexed, but didn't dare say so, and these difficulties served only to increase Ribaldos's love. He spent his whole time devising ways of seeing her: he dressed himself up as a monk, as a travelling saleswoman of ladies' clothing, as a puppeteer. All in vain: it wasn't enough to overcome Cosi-Sancta's resistance and more than enough to arouse her husband's suspicions. Had she come to an agreement with Ribaldos, they could easily have taken steps to prevent her husband from being suspicious. But she resisted her love, felt that her conscience was clear and managed to maintain the status quo – although she struggled to keep up appearances: her husband was convinced of her guilt.

So this very angry little man who imagined that his honour depended entirely on his wife's fidelity outrageously abused her and punished her because other men thought her beautiful. She found herself in the most horrible situation possible for a woman: unfairly accused and mistreated by a husband to whom she had remained faithful, while at the same time being torn by a passion that she was making every effort to resist.

She thought that if her lover were to cease pursuing her, her husband might stop treating her so harshly and that she might, with luck, be cured of her love once it had become so obviously impossible. With this in mind, she ventured to write this letter to Ribaldos:

*If you are a good man, I beg you to stop making me unhappy. Your love for me is exposing me to the suspicions and violence of my husband, my master, to whom I have given myself for the rest of my life. I wish to God that that were the only risk threatening me! For pity's sake, stop pursuing me! I entreat you by reason of that love which is tormenting us both and which can never bring you happiness.*

Poor Cosi-Sancta! She had not foreseen that a letter so tender yet so virtuous could have the completely opposite effect to that for which she had hoped. Her lover became so consumed by passion that he resolved to risk his life to see her.

Capito, who had the silly notion of wanting to be kept informed about everything and had some good spies, was told that Ribaldos had disguised himself as a Carmelite friar and was coming to beg for alms from his wife. He thought he was lost and that a Carmelite's gown was by far the greatest threat to a husband's honour; he posted some thugs to beat up Ribaldos and they did their job all too thoroughly. When he went into the house, these gentlemen set on him and, though he loudly protested that he was only an honest Carmelite friar and should not be treated so roughly, he was knocked out and, a fortnight later, he died from a blow he had received on the head. He was mourned by every wife in the town; Cosi-Sancta was inconsolable. Even Capito was annoyed, though for other reasons: he found himself landed in a very awkward situation.

Ribaldos was a relative of the proconsul who, being a Roman, wanted to exact exemplary punishment for the murder; and as he had in the past quarrelled with the presidium, he wasn't sorry to have a good reason for having one of the councillors hanged;

he was delighted that fate had decided that it would be Capito, who was certainly the vainest and most unbearably pretentious little pettifogger of them all.

So Cosi-Sancta had seen her lover murdered and was likely to see her husband hanged, purely as a result of being virtuous, since, as I've already pointed out, had she accepted Ribaldos's love, it would have been far easier to deceive her husband.

Thus some of the priest's predictions had been fulfilled, but Cosi-Sancta remembered the oracle and was desperately afraid that she would fulfil the rest. But after careful reflection, realizing that it's no use struggling against fate, she threw herself into the hands of Providence, which would lead her to its aim in the most honourable possible way.

The proconsul Acidynus was a libertine rather than a sybarite; he didn't waste time on preliminaries; he was a brutal, unceremonious, barrack-room macho, greatly feared in the provinces, whom all the women of Hippo had had dealings with, purely to avoid falling foul of him.

He sent for Cosi-Sancta; she arrived in tears, which made her look all the more appealing.

"Your husband is going to be hanged, madam," he said, "and his fate depends entirely upon you."

"I'd give my life to save him," she replied.

"No one is asking you for your life," the proconsul said.

"Then what am I to do?"

"I'm asking only for one night with you," replied the proconsul.

"That night is not mine to give; it belongs to my husband. I would give all my blood to save him, but my honour I cannot sacrifice."

"Suppose your husband agrees?"

"He is my master and everyone can do what he likes with his property. But I know my husband and he will never do what you suggest. He's a stubborn little man who'll certainly prefer to be hanged rather than have anyone else lay a hand on me."

"We'll see!" said the proconsul angrily, and immediately sent for the criminal. He gave him two options: be hanged or cuckolded. That was the only choice and he'd better make up his mind pretty smartly. But the little man still took a lot of persuading before doing what everyone would have done in his place. His wife had saved his life out of the kindness of her heart. This was the first of the three occasions.

That same day, her son fell ill with a most extraordinary disease, unfamiliar to any of the doctors in Hippo. The only doctor who knew anything about this mysterious illness lived in Aquila, several leagues away. At that time, doctors who practised in one town were forbidden to leave to practise in any other. Cosi-Sancta was forced to go herself with a brother whom she loved dearly. On the way, she was ambushed by brigands and the leader of these gentlemen took a fancy to her. They were on the point of killing her brother when he came over to her and said that if she were prepared to oblige him, he wouldn't be killed and they'd be allowed to go on their way for free. It was an urgent decision: she'd just saved the life of her husband, whom she didn't care for, and was about to lose her brother, of whom she was very fond; and she was also concerned about her son: there was not a moment to lose. She commended her soul to God, and did everything required. And this was the second of the three occasions.

She arrived in Aquila that same day and called on the doctor. He was that fashionable sort of doctor whom ladies send for when they have the vapours or when they have nothing wrong with them at all. Some of them confided in him, others became his lovers: as you see, a pleasant, obliging man, somewhat at odds, by the way, with a number of his colleagues at the faculty, about whom he told some most amusing stories when he was offered the chance.

Cosi-Sancta explained to him the symptoms of her son's illness and offered him a gold sestertius (a very large sum, worth about a thousand crowns or more in our currency).

"I don't want to be paid in that sort of money," the doctor replied, with a charming smile. "I would myself offer you everything I possess were you to allow yourself to be rewarded for all the remedies that you can offer me: if you were able to relieve the suffering that you are causing me, then I shall give your son back his health."

Cosi-Sancta thought this proposal more than a little bizarre, but Fate had accustomed her to accept strange things. And the doctor was an insistent man who would not accept any other form of payment for his services. It was impossible for Cosi-Sancta to consult her husband, and how could she let her son, whom she adored, die when all that was needed to save him was this small gesture? She was as good a mother as she was a sister and she was ready to pay the same price for his cure. This was the last of the three occasions.

She returned to Hippo with her brother who, throughout the whole journey, never ceased praising the courage she had shown in order to save his life.

And so, by being too virtuous, she had caused the death of her lover and the sentencing to death of her husband; by being more accommodating, she had saved the lives of her brother, her son and her husband. The people of Hippo felt that it was very important for every family to have such a wife and, after her death, made her a saint for having mortified her flesh in order to do good for the sake of her relatives. On her tombstone they engraved the inscription:

*A small sin to achieve a greater good.*

# Plato's Dream

P LATO WAS A GREAT DREAMER and people have gone on dreaming just as much ever since. He saw that humans had originally been comprised of two parts and that they'd been split into male and female as a punishment for their mistakes.

He'd proved that there can't be more than five perfect worlds because, mathematically, there are only five perfectly regular bodies. One of his great dreams was the *Republic*. He dreamt that wakefulness gives rise to sleep and sleep gives rise to wakefulness; another dream was that if you watched an eclipse of the sun otherwise than in a bowl of water, you'd be sure to lose your sight. In those days you could gain a great reputation by dreaming.

Here's one of his least interesting dreams. Apparently, the great Demiurge, the Creator of the world, the eternal Geometrician, after populating an infinite space with a countless number of globes, wanted to test the competence of the spirits who'd witnessed his works and gave each of them one small piece of matter to arrange, rather as Phidias or Zeuxis* would have given their pupils statues and pictures to produce – you must forgive me for comparing such petty things to such grand ones.

Demogorgon* was allotted a little scrap of mud which we know as *the earth* and when he'd arranged it in the way we see it today, he claimed to have produced a masterpiece; he thought he'd silenced any envy and was expecting nothing but praise, even from his fellow artists. He was greatly surprised to be greeted by boos.

One of them, a consummate hoaxer, sneered: "Oh yes, that's a really splendid piece of work you've produced: you've split your world into two and put a vast amount of water between the two hemispheres, so that they can't communicate with each other. Those at the two poles will freeze to death and those on the equator will die from the heat. You've carefully set up large sandy deserts so that anyone crossing them will die of hunger and thirst. I quite like your chickens, your sheep and your cows, but frankly I don't think much of your snakes and your spiders. Your onions and artichokes are very good, but I can't see the point of covering the earth with so many toxic plants, unless you intend to poison its inhabitants. What's more, you seem to have created thirty species of monkeys, even more species of dogs and only four or five kinds of man. It's true that you've endowed this last sort of animal with something you call *reason*, but let me tell you honestly that your reason is just too ridiculous and dangerously close to madness. In any case, it doesn't seem to me that you think very highly of that particular biped, because you've given it so many enemies and provided it with so few defences, so many illnesses and so few remedies, so many passions and so little wisdom. It seems that you don't want many of these animals to survive since, apart from all the dangers you've exposed them to, you've arranged things so cleverly that one day smallpox will regularly wipe out one tenth of their species and its big sister, syphilis, will poison the source of life in the remaining nine tenths. And as if that wasn't enough, you've worked everything so well that half the survivors will be busily going to law and the other half going to war. No doubt they'll all feel greatly obliged to you. Yes, you really have produced a masterpiece."

Demogorgon blushed: he was well aware that there were things in his work that were morally and physically wrong but still maintained that there was more good than bad in it.

"It's all very well for you to criticize me," he said, "but do you think it's all that easy to create an animal that's always reasonable, who's free and never abuses that freedom? Do you think that when you have to provide nine or ten thousand plants, it's easy to prevent some of them from being harmful? Do you imagine that, given a certain quantity of water, mud, sand and fire, you avoid having seas and deserts? You're laughing at me but, as you've finished making the planet Mars, let's have a look at what you've managed to do with your two big circles and the wonderful effect of your nights without a moon. We'll see if there are people there who aren't mad or ill."

So the genics examined Mars and pulled the clever fault-finder's own work to pieces. And they didn't spare the very thoughtful creator of Saturn either, and his colleagues who'd produced Jupiter, Mercury and Venus also came under attack as well, for one reason or another.

Massive volumes were printed and quite a few pamphlets as well. Songs were composed, jokes were made, people were ridiculing each other and things were turning nasty, until finally the Eternal Demiurge ordered all of them to stop.

"You've done some things that are good, some that are bad," he said. "This is because you're very intelligent and nobody is perfect; your works will only last a few hundred million years, after which, having learnt more, you'll do better. I'm the only one capable of creating something perfect and immortal."

Such was Plato's teaching to his disciples. And when he'd stopped talking, one of them said:

"And then you woke up."

# Micromegas

## A Philosophical Story

### Chapter I

*Journey by an Inhabitant of the Star* SIRIUS
*to the Planet* SATURN

IN ONE OF THE PLANETS that circle round the star Sirius
there lived a very bright young man whom I had the honour of
meeting during his recent journey to our little ant hill; his name
was Micromegas, a most suitable name for all great men. He was
about eight leagues tall, a league being thirty thousand geometric
feet, each measuring five feet.

Some algebraists, always happy to oblige, will at once pick
up their pens and work out that, as this inhabitant of Sirius
Micromegas was twenty-four thousand feet tall, from head to
foot, and that we earthly citizens are just about five feet and
that our globe is about nine hundred leagues in diameter, they'll
work out, as I was saying, that there can be no doubt at all
that the circumference of a globe which can produce such a tall
man must be exactly twenty-one million six hundred thousand

times larger than that of our tiny earth. There couldn't be anything more normal or more obvious: Nature's like that; and the princely states in Germany or Italy, some of which take only half a day to cross, when compared to the Turkish or Muscovite or Chinese empires, give a very poor idea of the prodigious differences that Nature has provided in every single one of its creatures.

Since His Excellency was so tall, our painters and sculptors will have no difficulty in agreeing that he must have measured about ten thousand feet round the waist – a very elegant figure.

His mind is one of the most cultured that exists; not only does he know a great number of things, he has invented some too. Before he was two hundred and fifty years old and still being taught, like everyone else, by the Jesuits of his planet, his formidable intelligence had enabled him to work out, by himself, more than fifty theorems of Euclid – eighteen more than Pascal,* who, after working out thirty-two, without really trying (according to his sister), later became a very ordinary geometrician and a really poor metaphysician.

Towards the end of his childhood – not quite four hundred and fifty years old – he dissected large numbers of those tiny Sirian insects – barely a hundred feet in diameter, quite impossible to see with ordinary microscopes. He wrote a very curious book about them which got him into a spot of trouble with the Mufti of Sirius, a tremendous nit-picker and extremely ignorant, who found propositions in the book that were suspect, offensive, rash, heretical or smacking of heresy, and launched vigorous proceedings against him: it was a question of whether the fleas of Sirius are, in sum and substance, of the same nature as the snails. Micromegas wittily defended himself and won all the women over to his side. This case went on for two hundred and twenty years. In the end, the mufti persuaded lawyers, who hadn't read the book, to condemn it, and the author was banned from the Court for eight hundred years. Micromegas wasn't greatly perturbed by being banned from a Court where pettiness and squabbling were the main order of the day.

He wrote a highly amusing song against the Mufti, which left the latter quite unmoved. In order to complete the development of his heart and mind, as the expression goes, Micromegas set out to travel from planet to planet. People who travel only by post-chaise or carriage will doubtless be amused by the vehicles they have up there, because on our miserable little mud heap we can't imagine anything unfamiliar to us. Our traveller had a marvellous knowledge of the law of gravity and the power of attraction and repulsion; he used them so efficiently that, with the help of the odd ray of sun and a convenient comet or two, he travelled with his entourage from one globe to the next like a bird flitting from one branch to the other. He shot through the Milky Way in a flash and I'm afraid I have to inform you that in that vast cluster of stars with which it is studded, he never saw that heavenly light of the empyrean which the illustrious vicar Derham* in England boasts of having seen through the gaps between the stars at the end of his telescope. Not that I'm claiming that the reverend gentleman couldn't have looked properly, God forbid! But Micromegas was there, on the spot; he's a keen observer and I have, of course, no desire whatsoever to contradict anyone.

After travelling around a good deal, Micromegas finally made a landing on Saturn. Although he'd become accustomed to seeing novelties, when he saw how tiny the globe and its inhabitants were, he couldn't suppress that smile of superiority which sometimes even the wisest of us can't manage to conceal. Saturn is in fact only nine hundred times larger than the Earth and the Saturnians themselves are only about 6,800 feet tall. At first, he and his companions rather joked about them (somewhat as an Italian musician will laugh at the music of Lully* when he visits France), but as our Sirian had an understanding nature, he quickly came to see that a thinking being may well not be ridiculous merely because he's only six thousand feet tall. At first, he came as a shock to the Saturnians but he soon got to know them. He formed a close friendship with the secretary of the Academy of Saturn, a very intelligent man who'd never had an original idea of his own but who made excellent summaries of other people's, was quite a good minor poet and very clever at sums. To satisfy my reader's curiosity, let me give you an account of a curious conversation Micromegas had one day with this secretary.

## Chapter II

*Conversation between a Sirian and a Saturnian*

A FTER HIS EXCELLENCY had lain down and the Secretary of the Academy had placed himself close to his face, Micromegas said:

"We must admit that Nature is extraordinarily varied."

"Yes," replied the secretary, "nature is like a flower bed whose flowers—"

"Oh, let's forget your flowers."

"It's like a group of blondes and brunettes," the secretary continued, "whose—"

"What have your brunettes got to do with me?"

"Well then, it's like a picture gallery which features—"

"No, no," said Micromegas, "Nature is just Nature. Why attempt to compare it with anything else?"

"In order to please you," the secretary replied.

"I don't want to be pleased," said the traveller. "I want to be informed. So, first of all, how many senses do the people living on this globe have?"

"Seventy-two," the academician replied, "and we're always complaining that we have so few. Our imagination outstrips our needs; we feel that with our seventy-two senses, seven moons and only one ring, there's still something lacking, and in spite of our curiosity and all the passions that come from having seventy-two senses, we find ourselves getting bored."

"I can well understand that feeling," said Micromegas, "for in our country we have nearly a thousand senses and we still have a vague longing, a feeling of unease which continually makes us realize that we're not really worth very much and that there might exist creatures more perfect than we are. I've travelled around quite a bit and seen people far inferior as well as greatly superior to us. But I've never met anyone who didn't want more than he really needed and have more needs than ways of satisfying them. One day perhaps I'll come to a country which doesn't lack anything, but up till now I've never received firm information about the existence of such a country."

The Saturnian and the Sirian both launched into endless conjectures on this subject, but after a good deal of ingenious and indecisive argument, they were forced to come down to hard facts.

"How long do you live?" enquired the Sirian.

"Oh dear, not very long," replied the little Saturnian.

"It's the same with us," replied Micromegas. "We're always complaining about it. It must be a law of nature."

"Yes, alas," agreed the Saturnian. "We live only about five hundred revolutions of the sun." (This corresponds to about fifteen thousand years of our time.) "So you can see that we die almost as soon as we're born. Our life is like a little dot, we last only for a moment and our globe is no larger than an atom. We scarcely have time to start learning something before death comes to cut short our existence. As for myself, I don't dare to make any plans; I feel like a small drop in the immense ocean. And I feel particularly ashamed when I'm with you: what a ridiculous figure I must seem in the world."

"If it weren't for the fact that you're a philosopher," said Micromegas, "I'd be afraid of making you feel even more distressed by telling you that we live seven times longer than you. But you well understand that when the time comes for us to return our body to the elements, giving life back to nature in another form, which we call dying, when this moment of metamorphosis comes, there's not the slightest difference between living for a day and living for an eternity. I've been to countries where people live a thousand times longer than in mine and I discovered that they still weren't happy. But there are sensible people everywhere who are able to accept their lot and give thanks to the great Author of Nature. He has scattered throughout the universe an immense number of varieties to create a single, admirable uniformity. For example, all thinking beings are different, but remain fundamentally the same because they have all been given desire and the power of thought. Matter can be found everywhere, but it takes on different attributes in different globes. How many attributes do you reckon to have in your form of matter?"

"If you mean those attributes without which we think our globe could not continue to exist in its present form," replied the Saturnian, "we reckon that there are three hundred, such as extent, impenetrability, motion, gravitation, divisibility and all the others."

"Apparently the Creator considered that small number of attributes adequate, in view of the small size of your domicile," said the celestial traveller. "I see everywhere how admirably wise he was: everywhere one notices differences, but they are carefully proportionate. You live on a small globe and its inhabitants are similarly small; you have few sensations; your matter has few attributes. It's all in the hands of Providence. What colour is your sun, when closely examined?"

"A very yellowish white," replied the Saturnian, "and when we split up one of its rays, we find it contains seven colours."

"Our sun is reddish," said the Sirian, "and we have thirty-nine primary colours. Among all the suns I've come across, not a single one resembles any other, just as with you there's not a single face which looks like anybody else's."

After asking several questions of this sort, he enquired how many fundamentally different substances the Saturnians calculated that they had and was told that there were about thirty, such as God, space, matter, beings occupying space who can feel, non-spatial beings who can think, beings who can interpenetrate and those who can't, and all the rest. The Sirian, whose star contained a thousand substances, greatly astonished his friend from Saturn when he told him that, on his travels, he'd discovered another three thousand.

Finally, after exchanging information about all the things they knew and those they didn't know, spending one whole revolution of the sun in their discussions, they agreed to launch out on a little philosophical trip together.

## Chapter III

*The Inhabitant of Sirius and the Inhabitant of Saturn
Set out on Their Philosophical Trip*

OUR TWO PHILOSOPHERS WERE ALL READY to launch themselves from Saturn into the atmosphere, equipped with a very nice selection of mathematical instruments, when the Saturnian's mistress, having got wind of their expedition, appeared, in tears, and remonstrated with him. She was a pretty little brunette, only 7,260 feet tall, but to compensate for her small stature she possessed many other charms.

"How cruel you are!" she cried. "After resisting you for 1,500 years, we've only been together for one hundred years and now you want to leave me to go off travelling with a giant from another world. Oh, I can see you're only interested in finding something new, you don't know what love means. If you were a true Saturnian you'd be faithful. Where will you go? What will you be looking for? Our five moons don't wander round like that, nor is our ring as changeable as you are. I've had enough of it all, I shall never fall in love with anyone again."

The philosopher gave her a hug and, being a philosopher, shared her tears, and the lady, having swooned, went off to console herself with a local dandy.

Meanwhile, our two explorers set off, first of all landing on Saturn's ring – which, as a distinguished inhabitant of our own little globe had cleverly surmised, was extremely flat. Next they moved from one moon to another. Close to the last one, a comet was going by, so they jumped onto it with their servants and all their equipment. After they'd travelled a hundred and fifty million leagues, they came across Jupiter's satellites and even landed on Jupiter itself and spent a year there, during which time they uncovered some superb secrets, which would be currently in press now had the gentlemen from the Inquisition not found one or two of the propositions rather difficult. But I've seen the manuscript in the library of the illustrious Archbishop of —— who gave me access to his books with a kindness and generosity beyond praise.

But to return to our travellers: after leaving Jupiter, they went on for about a hundred million leagues, passing by our own little planet Mars, which as you know is five times smaller than our tiny Earth; they saw its two little moons, which our astronomers have as yet failed to detect. I'm well aware that a Father Castel,* who doesn't understand Newton, will write, quite amusingly, to prove that these two moons don't exist, but I'm relying on people who base their arguments on analogy. Such good philosophers know how difficult it would be for Mars, so far from the sun, to manage without at least two moons. Be that as it may, our voyagers found Mars so small that they were afraid that there wouldn't be room for them to lie down, so they continued on their way like two travellers who, not prepared to risk a bad village inn, press on to the neighbouring town. But the Sirian and the Saturnian soon realized that they'd made a mistake, for they had to go on for a long time without finding anything, until at last they noticed a tiny gleaming object: it was the Earth and, for anyone coming from Jupiter, it looked pitiful. Nevertheless, not wanting to make any more mistakes, they decided to land. They left through the tail of the comet and, finding an aurora borealis handy, they got onto it and landed on the Earth on the south bank of the Baltic Sea on 5th July 1737 (NS).

## Chapter IV

### *What Happened to Them on Earth*

AFTER RESTING FOR A WHILE, they had a couple of mountains for breakfast, quite decently prepared by their servants, after which they set out to explore the little country they'd landed on. First, they went from north to south. The normal step of the Sirian was about three thousand feet; the Saturnian dwarf followed a long way behind, panting, because he had to take three steps to every one of the Sirian's. If one's allowed to make such a comparison, imagine a little lapdog keeping up with a captain of the guards of the King of Prussia who'd be about seven feet tall.

As these particular foreigners moved quite quickly, it took them only thirty-six hours to go round the world; the sun, or rather the earth, takes twenty-four hours to do that, but you mustn't forget that it's far easier to spin on your axis than walk on your feet. Anyway, they were now back where they'd started, having seen that little pool which we call the Mediterranean and that other little pond that encircles this tiny molehill and which we call the Great Ocean, whose waves never came more than halfway up the dwarf's legs and barely wet the other one's heel. On their way, they'd done everything possible, looking high and low, to see if the globe was inhabited, bending down, lying down, groping around everywhere. Their eyes and hands weren't adapted to finding those tiny creatures who crawl around on Earth, and they didn't feel the slightest sensation to lead them to suspect that we and all the other inhabitants of the world have the honour of existing.

At first, the dwarf, subject at times to making overhasty judgements, decided that there was nobody on Earth. His reason for thinking this was that he hadn't seen anyone. Micromegas politely pointed out that this was not a very sound argument.

"After all," he said, "you yourself, having such small eyes, can't see certain stars of the fiftieth magnitude that I can see quite distinctly. But can you therefore conclude that those stars don't exist?"

"But I did poke around carefully," replied the dwarf.

"But you didn't feel around properly."

"But this planet is so badly arranged," argued the dwarf. "It's so uneven and it seems to me such a silly shape. It's completely chaotic. Just look at all those little streams flowing in all directions, those lakes that are neither square nor round nor oval nor in any sort of regular shape. And what about all those bristly pointed grains which scratched my feet." He was referring to mountains. "And did you notice the irregular shape of the globe, flat on top, and how awkwardly it turns round the sun, so that those poles can never be cultivated? To tell you the truth, the reason why I think this place is uninhabited is that nobody in their senses would choose to live here."

"Well," retorted Micromegas, "perhaps there is nobody with any common sense living here. But, after all, the possibility exists that this place hasn't been made for no reason at all. You say that nothing here is regular because in Jupiter and Saturn everything is dead straight, but perhaps that's the very reason why things are a bit mixed up here. Didn't I tell you that in my travels I'd always met a great variety of things?"

The Saturnian had an answer to everything Micromegas said and their argument would have gone on for ages if, fortunately, in the heat of their discussion, Micromegas hadn't broken the thread of his diamond necklace. The diamonds fell down onto the ground: they were very pretty little rough-cut stones of varying sizes, the largest of which weighed four hundred pounds and the smallest only fifty. The dwarf picked up a few of them and, holding them close to his eyes, noticed that, through the way they had been cut, they made excellent microscopes. He selected a little one, about a hundred and sixty feet in diameter and put it to his eye. Micromegas picked one up as well, about two thousand five hundred feet round. They made excellent microscopes, but at first they couldn't see anything; they needed adjusting. Finally, the Saturnian saw something almost imperceptible moving between two waves in the Baltic: it was a whale. He very cleverly caught it with his little finger, placed it on his thumbnail and showed it to the Sirian, who again started laughing at the extremely diminutive nature of the inhabitants of the Earth. But convinced that our globe is inhabited, the Saturnian immediately came to the conclusion that it was inhabited only by whales and as he loved speculating, he began to work out how such minute atoms were able to move, if they could have ideas, willpower, free will. Micromegas was quite at a loss: he examined the animal very patiently and decided there was no way he could imagine its having a soul. So our travellers were just beginning to think that our world is mindless when, with the help of their microscope, they detected something larger than a whale floating on the Baltic. At that time, as we all know, a swarm of philosophers were on their way back from the Arctic Circle, where they'd been to make certain observations that nobody had thought of making before. The papers reported that their ship had run aground on the coast of the Gulf of Bothnia and that they had a very narrow escape; but, here below, we never really know the true story. I'm going to give you a simple, honest account of what actually happened, without inventing anything of my own – and that's no mean feat for a historian.

## Chapter V

*Our Two Voyagers Have Experiences and Hear Arguments*

MICROMEGAS GENTLY reached out towards the place where the object seemed to be, stretched out two fingers, drew them back in case he'd made a mistake and finally brought them together, cleverly catching hold of the ship carrying these learned gentlemen and once more placed the object on his nail, very gently so as not to crush it.

"This is an animal quite different from the first one," said the dwarf from Saturn. The Sirian put this alleged animal on the palm of his hand. The passengers and crew, imagining that they had been caught up in a hurricane and deposited on some sort of rock, all move into action: the crew pick up some wine barrels, throw them onto Micromegas's hand and jump overboard after them; the geometricians pick up their quadrants, their sectors and their girls from Lapland and clamber down onto the Sirian's fingers. So active were they that he eventually felt a tickling in his finger: a sharp steel-pointed shaft which was being thrust a foot deep into his flesh. The sensation made him think that something must have come out of the little object he was holding, though at the time he didn't pay any further attention to the matter. Their microscope, which could barely pick out a whale or a ship, could hardly see something as imperceptible as a human being. I'm not trying to offend anyone's vanity, but I do feel obliged to ask any self-important persons among you to share with me a small comment: assuming the height of a normal man to be about five feet, we don't make any greater impression on earth than would be made by any animal roughly the six hundred thousandth of an inch on a ball ten feet round. Just think of something capable of holding the earth in its hand and possessing organs roughly proportionate in size to ours – and these things may exist in large numbers – then I ask you to imagine what they would think of our battles which cost us a couple of villages.

I've no doubt that, if some captain of these very tall grenadiers ever reads this work, he'll increase the height of his troopers' hats by at least two feet, but let me warn him that it'll be a waste of time and that he and those like him will never be anything but infinitesimal.

So how terribly clever our Sirian philosopher had to be to catch sight of these tiny atoms I've just mentioned! When those Leeuwenhoek and Hartsoeker were the first to see – or thought they saw – human sperm, their discovery was far less amazing.* How delighted Micromegas was when he saw those little machines actually moving about, when he examined all their little tricks and followed all their operations. He kept exclaiming and excitedly handed his microscope to his companion.

"I can see them!" they both exclaimed together. "Can't you see them carrying something on their backs, bending down and then straightening up?"

Their hands were trembling with delight at the sight of such novel objects, but also for fear of losing them. And the Saturnian, who had been so distrustful at first, now became too credulous, for he thought he was seeing them busily engaging in the propagation of their species.

"Aha!" he cried, "I've caught Nature in the act!"

He was being misled by appearances, as happens all too often, whether you're using a microscope or not.

## Chapter VI

### *The Things that Happened to Them with Men*

MICROMEGAS WAS A BETTER OBSERVER than the dwarf, and he could see quite plainly that these atoms were talking to each other. He pointed this out to his companion who, while ashamed at being mistaken over the act of propagation, refused to believe that such a species could communicate ideas to each other. But like the Sirian, he was endowed with the gift of tongues and, not being able to hear these atoms speaking to each other, he concluded that they weren't talking. In any case, how could these imperceptible atoms possess organs of speech and what would they have to say? In order to talk, you have to think, more or less, but if they were thinking, they would have to possess the equivalent of a soul, and it seemed absurd to think that such a species could have one.

"But only a moment ago," the Sirian said, "you thought they were making love. Do you think one can make love without thinking and without uttering a single word or, at least, making oneself understood? And anyway, do you think it's more difficult to produce an argument than to produce a child? For my part, I think both these things are very great mysteries."

"I'm going to stop denying or accepting anything," said the dwarf. "I'm not going to dare have any opinions any more. We must try and examine these insects and we can discuss it all later."

"Well said!" replied Micromegas and immediately took out a pair of nail scissors and cut off a piece of his thumbnail, which he turned into a sort of speaking trumpet, a sort of gigantic funnel, one end of which he stuck into his ear. The weakest of voices produced a vibration in the curved piece of nail, so that by this device the philosopher from outer space was able to hear perfectly the buzzing of the insects below. He took a few hours to distinguish words and then he understood the French. The dwarf did the same, though it wasn't quite so easy for him. The voyagers were growing more and more surprised: these mites were talking quite sensibly; they found it impossible to explain this quirk of nature and you can understand how impatient they were to get into conversation with these atoms, though the dwarf was afraid that their thunderous voices, particularly Micromegas's, might deafen these small creatures and prevent them from being understood. They had to reduce their volume. They put a kind of small toothpick into their mouths and pointed the sharp ends of them towards the ship. Micromegas was holding the dwarf on his knee and the ship on one of his nails. He bent over and spoke very, very gently. After taking all these precautions and quite a few more, he began:

"Invisible insects! The hand of your Creator has chosen to bring you to life in the depths of the infinitely small, and I thank him for having deigned to reveal to me secrets that seemed to me impenetrable. They may not deign to look at you at my court, but I myself hold no one in contempt and I offer you my protection."

Nobody could have been more surprised than these tiny specks on hearing these words. They had no idea where they were coming from. The boat's almoner started reciting exorcism prayers, the sailors started to swear and the philosophers started working out a system. Despite all their systems, they still hadn't the slightest idea of what was happening. The dwarf from Saturn, who had a quieter voice, briefly explained the sort of species they were dealing with. He told them about their travels from Saturn, who Monsieur Micromegas was, and after expressing sympathy for them, since they were so small, he asked them if they had always been in such a miserable state, bordering indeed on annihilation, what they were doing on a globe which appeared to be inhabited only by whales, if they were happy, if they were able to procreate, if they had souls and other questions of a similar nature.

One of the group, bolder than his fellow humans and fond of arguing, was shocked to hear someone doubting whether he had a soul, and after adjusting a sight vane on his quadrant and taking a couple of readings, finally took one more and then said:

"So you imagine, sir, that since you are six thousand feet from top to toe, you are—"

"Six thousand feet!" exclaimed the dwarf. "Heavens above! How can he know my height? Six thousand feet! He's got it right; that atom has actually measured me, to within an inch! He's a geometrician! And I, who can only see him through a microscope, I myself don't know how tall he is!"

"Yes, I did measure you and I'll measure your big companion as well."

The offer was accepted and His Excellency lay down flat on the ground, because otherwise his head would have been lost in the clouds. And our philosophers stuck a large tree into an aperture that Dr Swift would have mentioned quite explicitly but which I, having great respect for the ladies, shall not venture to name. Then, with the help of a series of triangles joined together, they calculated that what they could see was a young man 120,000 feet tall.

Then Micromegas spoke:

"More and more do I realize that you must not judge anything by appearances. God has given intelligence to substances that seem so contemptible, for whom creating the infinitely small is no more difficult than creating the infinitely large, and if it is possible that there are beings even smaller than these, they may have a mind superior to that of those superb animals that I've seen in space, one of whose feet would suffice to cover the whole of this globe on which I've landed."

One of the philosophers replied that he could indeed imagine that there are certainly intelligent beings smaller than man. He did not tell him about Virgil's fables on the subject of bees but what the Swammerdam had discovered and what Réaumur* had been dissecting. Finally, he explained to him that there are animals which are for bees what bees are for man and what the Sirian himself was for those animals he'd been talking about and what those large animals were for other substances compared with which they would seem as small as atoms. The conversation was gradually becoming interesting and Micromegas spoke again.

## Chapter VII

*A Conversation with Men*

"INTELLIGENT ATOMS THAT YOU ARE, in whom the Eternal Being has been pleased to manifest his might and skill, you must doubtless enjoy the purest of pleasures on your globe, since you contain so little matter and seem to consist of nothing but spirit. You must spend your lives in loving and thinking, which is the true life of blessed spirits. Nowhere have I seen true happiness, but assuredly it must be here?'

When they heard these words, the philosophers all shook their heads and one of them, more honest than the rest, frankly admitted that, apart from a few people whom nobody thought very highly of, everybody else was mad, evil or unhappy.

"We have in us more matter than we need to do a great deal of harm," he said, "assuming, of course, that evil is caused by matter, and too much mind, assuming that evil comes from the mind. For example, do you know that at this very moment there are a hundred thousand idiots of our species called Russians and wearing caps, killing a hundred thousand similar animals called Turks and wearing turbans, unless they are being massacred by them? What is more, they've been doing it since time immemorial."

The Sirian shuddered and asked what might be the reason for these horrible disputes between such petty little animals.

"It's all about a few tiny heaps of mud no larger than your heel," replied the philosopher, "and there's not one of these millions of humans getting their throats slit who wants to have a spoonful of the mud. It's just a question whether it should belong to a certain man called a Sultan or another one called, God alone knows why, Caesar or Tsar. And neither of them has even seen or ever will see this little speck of earth which they call Crimea, nor have hardly any of these little animals busy cutting each other's throats ever seen the animal on whose behalf they're doing it."

"You poor unhappy wretches!" exclaimed the Sirian indignantly. "How can one even imagine such atrocious savagery? In just three steps I could stamp out this whole ant hill of stupid murderers, and I'm tempted to do it."

"It's not worth your trouble," the human replied, "they'll manage to do it perfectly well themselves without your help. Let me tell you that in ten years' time not one per cent of those wretched people will have survived, even if they never draw a sword: famine or exhaustion or self-indulgence will have wiped out almost all of them. In any case, it's not they who should be punished but that barbarous lot sitting tucked comfortably away in their offices, who while digesting a good meal will order a million men to be massacred, after which they'll solemnly offer thanks to God."

The visitor from outer space was moved to pity for this tiny human race in which he was discovering such amazing contrasts.

"As you belong to this small group of wise men," he said, "and apparently don't go about killing each other for money, may I ask how you yourselves spend your time?"

"We dissect flies," replied the philosopher, "we measure lines, we put numbers together, we agree on two or three points which we're able to understand and we disagree on two or three thousand others which we don't understand."

It immediately occurred to the Sirian and the Saturnian that it would be fascinating to ask these thinking atoms what they did agree on.

"By your calculation, how many degrees are there between the Dog Star and the larger of the two Gemini?"

They answered with one voice:

"Thirty-two."

"And how far is it from here to the Moon?"

"Sixty-two and a half diameters of the Earth, in round numbers."

He now tried to catch them out:

"What's the weight of your air?"

They all said that air weighed nine hundred times less than the same volume of the lightest water and nine thousand times less than the gold in a ducat. The little dwarf from Saturn was so surprised by their replies that he was tempted to think that these people whom, only a quarter of an hour ago, he'd suspected of not having a soul, were magicians.

Finally, Micromegas asked:

"As you know so much about the world outside you, no doubt you have an even better idea of what is inside you. Tell me about your soul and how you form your ideas."

As before, the philosophers all replied simultaneously, but this time they were all saying something different. The oldest of them mentioned Aristotle, another man spoke of Descartes, someone else of Malebranche, yet another of Leibniz and then Locke's name was heard.* Another old disciple of Aristotle said confidently, in a loud voice, that the soul was an entelechy capable of attaining perfection and a reason through which it has the power to become what it is; and that this was what Aristotle had expressly declared on page 633 of the Louvre edition; and then he quoted some Greek.

"I'm afraid my Greek's not very good," said the giant.

"Neither is mine," replied the minuscule philosopher.

"Then why are you quoting Aristotle to me in Greek?" enquired the Sirian.

"Because it's a good idea to quote something you don't understand in the language you understand least well," the learned man replied.

The follower of Descartes said:

"The soul is a pure spirit that, in its mother's belly, picked up every metaphysical idea that has ever existed and, when it came out of there, was obliged to go to school and learn all over again everything which it knew so well already and won't ever know again."

"So it wasn't worth the trouble," commented the giant animal, "for your soul to know so much in your mother's womb and be so ignorant when you'd started growing a beard. But what do you understand by the word soul or spirit?"

"Don't ask me," replied the thinker, "I've no idea. They say it's something that isn't material."

"But then at least you know what matter is?"

"Of course," the man replied. "For example, that stone is grey and has a certain shape; it's heavy, divisible and three-dimensional."

"Well," the Sirian said, "that thing that seems to you capable of being divided, heavy and grey, would you tell me exactly what it is? You've mentioned some of its attributes, but do you know what its essence is?"

"No, I don't," replied the man.

"So you don't know what matter is either."

Then Micromegas spoke to another philosopher poised on his thumb and asked him what his soul was and what it did.

"Nothing at all," this man replied; he was a follower of Malebranche. "God does everything for me; I see everything in Him, I do everything through Him and I don't play any part at all."

"So it might just as well not exist," said the wise Sirian.

"And what about you, my friend," he said to a follower of Leibniz, "what sort of a soul do you think you have?"

"It's a needle that indicates the time while my body is ringing its bells – or, if you prefer, it rings the bells while my body is showing the time; my soul is the mirror of the universe and my body is the border of the mirror. It's perfectly clear."

A small follower of Locke was standing next to him and when finally he was asked the same question, he replied:

"I don't know how I think, but I do know that I've never been able to think without being able to use my senses. I have no doubt that there are immaterial and intelligent substances, but I doubt very much if it's impossible for God to convey thought to matter. I revere the eternal force, it's not for me to limit it; I make no assertions, I'm content to believe that there are more things possible than we think."

The animal from Sirius smiled and did not think that this last speaker was the least wise, while the Saturnian dwarf would have embraced this follower of Locke but for the discrepancy in size. But unfortunately a very diminutive animal wearing the square hat of a theologian from the Sorbonne happened to be there, and he chose to interrupt all the little philosophical animals by saying that he had the complete answer to this secret, which was in the *Summa Theologica* of St Thomas Aquinas,* and, looking haughtily up at the two celestial giants, he asserted that they, the worlds they lived in, their stars, everything, was solely for the use of man. On hearing this, our two travellers fell into each other's arms, trying to stifle that inextinguishable laughter which Homer calls the laughter of the gods;* their shoulders and bellies heaved so convulsively that the ship which the Sirian had on his nail fell into the pocket of the Saturnian's breeches and, being friendly creatures, they both spent a long time looking for it, and having found it they settled the crew comfortably back on board.

The Sirian picked up the little mites again, still treating them kindly, though inwardly rather annoyed that such infinitely small creatures were so almost infinitely arrogant. He promised to produce a splendid volume of philosophy, written specially for them, which would tell them everything about everything, and he did in fact give it to them before leaving. They took it to the Academy of Sciences in Paris, but when the secretary opened it, he found nothing but blank pages.

"That's just what I suspected!" he said.

# The Way of the World

## Babouc's Vision

### AS TOLD BY HIMSELF

## Chapter I

A MONG THE GENII who preside over the empires of this world, Ituriel ranks among the highest; his dominion is in Upper Asia. One morning, he went down to the dwelling of the Scythian Babouc, on the banks of the Oxus, and addressed him in these words: "Babouc, the monstrous excesses of the Persians have aroused our wrath: yesterday, an assembly of the genii of Upper Asia met to decide whether Persepolis should be punished or destroyed. You are to go to that city, examine it thoroughly and give me a full and true report, so that I may decide whether to force it to reform itself or to exterminate it."

"But I have never been to Persepolis, my lord," said Babouc humbly, "nor do I know anyone there."

"All the better," replied the angel. "You will be impartial and Heaven has granted you a sharp mind. For my part, I shall endow you with the ability to inspire confidence. Leave now, look, listen, observe and have no fear: you will be well received wherever you go."

Babouc got on to his camel and departed, with his servants. A few days later, on the plains of Sennaar, he came upon the Persian army on its way to fight the Indian army. Seeing a soldier who was standing apart from the main body, he asked him what the war was about. "Damned if I know," the private replied. "It's nothing to do with me. My job is to earn my living by killing or being killed. It doesn't matter to me what army I'm serving in. In fact, I've half a mind to go over to the Indian army tomorrow, because I've heard they pay you nearly half a copper drachma a day more than these miserable Persians. You'd better go and ask the captain why we're fighting."

Babouc slipped him a small tip and went into the camp, where he soon made the acquaintance of a captain. He asked him the reason for the fighting. "How on earth should I know?" replied the captain. "Why should such highfalutin matters have any importance for me? I live miles away from Persepolis, I hear that war's been declared, I immediately abandon my family and go off to seek my fortune or get killed, as we've always done, seeing that we've nothing else to do."

"But your brother officers?" asked Babouc. "Don't they know anything more about it?"

"No," the captain replied. "Only our senior commanders, the satraps, know why we're slitting each other's throats."

Babouc was astounded, went off to meet these senior officers and wormed his way into their confidence. Finally, one of them said: "The reason for this war, which has been devastating Asia for the last twenty years, goes back originally to a quarrel between one of the eunuchs of one of the wives of the Great Shah of Persia and an office clerk of the Great King of India. It concerned a particular due worth roughly a thirtieth of a daric. The prime minister of the Indians and our own prime minister very properly supported the rights of their masters. Hard words were exchanged and both sides launched a campaign involving a million soldiers, which requires four hundred thousand recruits every year. You see more and more fires, murders, ruins and general devastation everywhere you look. The whole universe is suffering; war is being waged mercilessly. Our prime minister and the prime minister of the Indians often protest that they're acting only to ensure the general welfare of mankind, and every time they protest there are always a few more towns destroyed and provinces plundered."

The next day, as there was a rumour that peace was about to be signed, the Persian and Indian generals hurriedly joined battle; the fighting was bloody and Babouc witnessed all its mistakes and all its horrors. He saw manoeuvres ordered by satraps doing their utmost to bring about their own leader's defeat. He saw officers being killed by their own troops; he saw soldiers finishing off their wounded dying comrades in order to snatch a few bloody, tattered, muddy rags of clothing. He went into the hospitals for the wounded, most of whom died through the callous indifference of those whom the King of Persia was paying good money to care for them. "Are these men or wild beasts?" exclaimed Babouc. "Oh, I can see that Persepolis will be destroyed!"

Pondering these thoughts, he came into the Indian camp and, as had been foretold, he was made equally welcome there, but here too he saw abuses being committed similar to those which had so horrified him among the Persians. "Ha!" he said to himself. "If the angel Ituriel wants to exterminate the Persians, then the angel of the Indians must also destroy the Indians."

Later, after gaining further information about what had happened in both armies, he learnt of noble, compassionate, unselfish acts which amazed and delighted him. "How inscrutable human beings are!" he exclaimed. "How can one be so vile and so noble, so good and so evil?"

Meanwhile, peace had been signed. The leaders of the two armies, neither of whom had been victorious in the course of causing so much bloodshed among their fellow humans, to further their own interests, now returned to intrigue at court to receive rewards for their services. Peace was celebrated by public proclamation, announcing that henceforth happiness and goodwill would reign on earth.

"Praised be the Lord," said Babouc. "Innocence will now be restored in all its purity to Persepolis, which will not now be destroyed, as those horrid genii had wished. Let us hasten without delay to visit this capital of Asia."

## Chapter II

H E CAME INTO THIS IMMENSE CITY by its old eastern gate, a disgustingly rough and primitive structure. This whole part of the town showed the influence of the times in which it was built; in spite of the stubbornness with which men praise the old at the expense of the modern, we have to admit that first attempts of any sort are somewhat rough.

Babouc joined the throng of people, which consisted of the dirtiest and ugliest of both sexes, as it surged confusedly into a vast, gloomy enclosure. The persistent hum and continual movement, the sight of people giving money to others in order to get a seat, led him to assume that he was in a market where they were selling straw-seated chairs, but when he saw women fall on their knees and pretend to be looking straight ahead while casting a sly glance at the men beside them, he became aware that he was in a temple. The high vault was reverberating to the sound of wild, shrill, raucous, inarticulate voices, like the braying of asses responding to the call of the herdsman's horn on the plains of Poitou. He stuck his fingers into his ears, but was tempted to plug his eyes and his nose as well when he saw workers carrying crowbars and shovels entering the temple. They moved a large stone and dug out some foul-smelling soil which they scattered around; then they placed the body of a dead man in the hole and put back the stone.

"Heavens above!" exclaimed Babouc. "They bury their dead in the place where they worship their God! So their temples are paved with corpses. I'm no longer surprised that Persepolis suffers from all sorts of pestilential plagues. These decaying bodies and the foul state in which they live all crammed together in one place are enough to infect the whole globe. What a horrid city Persepolis is! The angels must be wanting to destroy it in order to replace it by one more beautiful and populate it with people who aren't so filthy. Providence doubtless has its reasons: we must let it proceed with its work."

## Chapter III

MEANWHILE THE SUN was approaching its zenith. Babouc had to go to the other end of the city to call on a lady, whose husband, a Persian officer, had given him some letters to deliver. Before doing so, Babouc strolled around Persepolis; he saw other temples, better built and more decorative, filled with polite people and harmonious music; he saw public fountains which, even though badly situated, were strikingly beautiful; public squares where the greatest earlier rulers of Persia had been recreated in bronze statues, and other squares where he heard the public calling out: "When shall we see in this square our beloved master?" He admired the fine bridges crossing the river, the superb and convenient quaysides, the palaces on both banks, an immense building to house thousands of old soldiers, wounded yet victorious, who every day gave thanks to the god of armies. Finally, he came to the house of the lady who was expecting him, as well as a number of other gentlemen, as guests for dinner.

Her house was spotless and elegant, the meal delicious, the hostess young, beautiful, witty and enchanting and her guests were worthy of her. Babouc kept saying to himself: "The angel Ituriel is talking nonsense. How could he think of destroying such a charming city?"

## Chapter IV

HOWEVER, HE NOTICED that his hostess who, on his arrival, had asked lovingly after her husband, towards the end of the meal was talking even more lovingly to a young magus. He saw a judge, in the presence of his wife, openly flirting with a widow who had indulgently placed her hand round the judge's neck while stretching her other hand in the direction of a very handsome and very modest young citizen. The judge's wife was the first to leave the table to go and talk to her spiritual adviser in the next room; he had been expected for dinner but had arrived late. He was an eloquent man and spoke with such conviction and so unctuously that when the judge's wife came back, her eyes were tearful and flushed, she was swaying on her feet and her voice trembled.

Seeing this, Babouc began to be afraid that Ituriel might be right. That very day, the gift he had been granted to inspire confidence in others enabled him to discover the secrets of his hostess, who confessed that she was fond of the young magus and assured him that in every house of Persepolis he would discover similar situations to those he'd seen in hers. Babouc concluded that such a society was not worthy to survive and that every house in Persepolis must be racked by conflict, jealousy, thoughts of vengeance; that blood and tears must be shed every day; that husbands would certainly be killing – or be killed by – their wives' lovers and that it was very sensible of Ituriel to destroy at once such a completely evil and irreparably debauched city.

## Chapter V

PLUNGED IN SUCH GRIEVOUS THOUGHTS, he found that he was standing in front of a door where a man, soberly dressed in black, was asking the young judge, humbly, in a serious voice, if he might speak with him. Without standing up or looking at him, the judge, disdainfully, without paying him the slightest attention, tossed him some papers and told him he could go. Babouc asked the mistress of the house who this man was. She whispered to him: "He's one of the cleverest lawyers in town; he's been studying law for fifty years. The judge, who's been in charge for only two days and is only twenty-five years old, gives him a summary of any case that he's due to judge and hasn't yet looked into."

"That young scatterbrain is very wise to seek the advice of an experienced old man," said Babouc, "but how is it that it isn't the old lawyer himself who's the judge in charge of the case?"

"You must be joking," she replied. "People who've grown old toiling away in subordinate positions never reach the top. That young man has been made a judge because he has a rich father.

Here you can buy the right to hold a high post just as you buy a piece of land."

"What a monstrous and unhappy country!" exclaimed Babouc. "All I can see are the depths of evil."

As he was expressing his horror and amazement at such conduct, a young soldier who had just returned from the wars said to him:

"Why shouldn't legal posts be available to buy? I myself paid for the right to risk my life commanding two thousand men. This year alone it cost me a good forty thousand gold darics to sleep outside on the ground for thirty nights in a row wearing only my red uniform and being wounded twice by arrows – wounds I'm still suffering from. If I ruin myself to serve the Shah – whom, by the way, I've never seen – surely a judge can pay something to have the pleasure and privilege of giving a hearing to people asking for justice?"

Babouc was exasperated and felt that a country where high offices dealing with peace and war were put up for auction could only be condemned, rather hastily concluding that nobody in such a country could possibly understand the meaning of war or justice and that their hateful system of government would inevitably lead them to exterminate themselves even if Ituriel didn't.

His low opinion of them became even lower when a large man came in and, after greeting the assembled company in a very friendly manner, went over to the young officer and said: "I'm afraid I can only let you have fifty thousand darics, because this year I've only got three hundred thousand from the imperial customs duties." On enquiring, Babouc learnt that this man who was complaining at having received so little was one of the forty commoners who had a leasehold, like little kings, on the revenues of the state, giving a fraction of it back to the Shah.

## Chapter VI

AFTER DINNER, BABOUC WENT into one of the city's grandest temples and sat down with a group of men and women who'd come because they'd nothing better to do. A magus appeared on an extremely high piece of equipment and delivered an eloquent address on vice and virtue, carefully dividing into distinctive categories things that didn't need to be divided. He systematically proved things that required no proof; he taught his audience things that everyone already knew. He spoke, expressing passionate ideas with complete indifference, and when he left he was sweating and out of breath. The assembled company then woke up and thought that they'd been taught something. Babouc said to himself: "That was a man who was doing his best to bore two or three hundred of his fellow citizens, but that's not a reason to destroy the whole of Persepolis."

After leaving the temple, he was taken to see a grand public festival which took place every day in a sort of basilica at the back of which you could see a palace, the most beautiful women of the city and the most important satraps in orderly rows and forming so splendid a show that at first Babouc thought that he was watching the festival itself. Two or three persons who seemed to be kings or queens appeared in the vestibule of the palace; they spoke in tones very different from ordinary people, in carefully modulated, harmonious and sublime voices. Nobody went to sleep, everyone was listening silently, with rapt attention, a silence interrupted only by the spontaneous expression of their feelings or their admiration. The duties of kings, the love of virtue, the danger of passion were expressed so vividly, in such a touching manner, that Babouc was moved to tears. He had no doubt that these heroes and heroines, these kings and queens were the true voice of the Persian empire; he even thought to himself that he should advise Ituriel to come and listen to them, convinced that seeing such things would reconcile him, once and for all, to the city.

As soon as the celebration was over, Babouc wanted to see this queen who had delivered such a pure and noble message in this palace. He was taken to meet Her Majesty: he was escorted up a narrow staircase to the second floor and shown into a poorly furnished apartment, where he found a badly dressed woman who said to him, in a noble and pathetic voice:

"My profession as a queen doesn't give me enough to live on; one of the princes whom you saw has made me pregnant and I'm soon going to have his child. I'm short of money and if I don't have money, I shan't be able to have the child." Babouc gave her a hundred darics, saying to himself: "If that is the only thing wrong in this city, Ituriel would be mistaken to be so angry."

From there he went on to spend the evening with some dealers in expensive and useless luxury goods, in the company of an acquaintance, an intelligent man; he bought something which took his fancy, paying much more than it was worth. On returning to his friend's house, the latter told Babouc how much he had been overcharged. Babouc wrote down the dealer's name to inform Ituriel when he came to punish the city. As he was doing this, the dealer himself came in to return Babouc's purse, which he had inadvertently left behind in the shop.

"How is it possible," exclaimed Babouc, "for you to behave so honestly and generously when you had no scruples in charging me four times the value of those baubles I bought from you?"

"There's not one dealer in the city who wouldn't have returned your purse," replied the dealer. "But you were being misled when you were told that I was charging you four times too much: it was ten times too much, and you'll see that if you want to resell them in a month's time you'll not even get that tenth. But that's absolutely fair and reasonable: the price of such paltry things is fixed by passing fads – and those fads enable me to give work to a hundred people; they've provided me with a fine house, a comfortable chariot and horses to draw it. They promote industry, which helps money to circulate and creates pleasure and prosperity. And I sell these trifles to neighbouring countries for much more than I charge you and thereby benefit the Persian empire."

Babouc pondered for a while and then crossed the dealer's name off the list of criminals.

## Chapter VII

STILL VERY UNCERTAIN as to what was to be done to Persepolis, Babouc went to consult the magi and the men of letters: the first concerned themselves with religion, the second with wisdom, and he felt sure that the former would obtain forgiveness for the rest of the population. The very next morning he arranged to be taken to a theological college. The archimandrite confided to him that he was receiving a hundred thousand crowns a year for having made a vow of poverty and that, having vowed to remain humble, he was in control of quite a considerable domain. He then passed Babouc over to a little friar to do him the honours.

While this friar was showing him all the splendours of this house devoted to contrition, the rumour spread that he'd been sent to reform all these various institutions and he immediately received numerous memoranda, each of which said, in substance: "Keep us and destroy all the rest". According to their apologia all these societies were essential, and according to their accusations they all deserved to be abolished. He was amazed to learn that in order to provide universal enlightenment, there was not one that did not demand to be in complete control. Then a little man who was half a magus came to see him and said: "I can see that the great work is about to be accomplished; Zoroaster has returned to earth; girls are full of prophecies of his return as they nip themselves with pincers in front and whip themselves from behind. This is how we ask for your protection against the Grand Lama."

"What?" exclaimed Babouc, "Against this great royal pontiff who reigns in Tibet?"

"That's the man."

"Are you at war with him? Are you raising armies against him?"

"No, but he says that man is free and that we do not believe at all. We're writing lots of little books attacking him and he's not reading them. He's hardly even heard of us; he's merely had us condemned, in the same way as the owner orders the trees in his gardens to be lopped."

Babouc trembled at the thought of such wild ideas in the heads of men who professed to be wise and of the intrigues of those who had renounced the world, of the ambition, pride and cupidity of those who were preaching humility and unselfishness. His conclusion was that Ituriel had every reason to destroy such a horrible breed of men.

## Chapter VIII

HE WENT HOME AND ASKED for a few books to read to cheer himself up. He also invited some men of letters to dinner, in order to have some pleasant company. Twice as many turned up as he'd invited, like wasps looking for honey. These parasites quickly set about eating and drinking. They were full of praise for two sorts of writers: dead ones and themselves; they didn't have a good word for their contemporaries – excepting their host. If anyone said something witty, they looked away and sadly bit their lips because they hadn't thought of it themselves. They were more outspoken than the magi, because they weren't aiming so high. Everyone there was doing their best to obtain some menial post – to enjoy the reputation of being someone important; they were openly exchanging insults which they thought displayed their wit. They had a vague idea of Babouc's mission. One of them asked him, in an undertone, to exterminate an author who hadn't shown him adequate praise five years ago. Someone else asked him to get rid of a man who never laughed at his comedies and one man asked him to abolish the Academy because he'd never managed to be elected to it. When the meal was over, they all went off separately, since not one of them could abide any of the others or even talk to them, except when they were some rich man's guests. Babouc concluded that there would be little lost if all this riff-raff disappeared in the great destruction.

## Chapter IX

A S SOON AS HE WAS RID OF THEM, he started to read his new books. He could recognize the hand of his guests. It was the scandal sheets that made him most angry, full of cheap jokes, inspired by base envy and greed: pusillanimous, tasteless satire in which you spare the vulture and carve up the dove; novels showing no imagination, portraying women the author had never met.

Babouc flung all this miserable rubbish into the fire and went out for an evening stroll. He was introduced to an old writer who had chosen not to add to the large number of parasites who had been his guests; this author always avoided the crowd, knew what men were, used his knowledge, discreetly, in his works. Babouc sadly confided in him what he'd been reading and seeing.

"You've been reading rubbish," the author said. "It's always the bad things which proliferate, while good things are scarce in any age or any country. You've hosted the dregs of pedantry, because in every profession it's the most worthless who have the least shame in flaunting themselves. The truly wise are quiet, retiring, and keep to themselves. There are still books worth reading and people worth knowing in Persepolis."

While he was talking, he was joined by another writer and they had such a pleasant, instructive and wide-ranging conversation together, so free from prejudice and rancour, so full of high principles that Babouc confessed that he had never heard anything of that sort before. "Ituriel," he said to himself, "would surely be pitiless to wish to harm such men."

However, though reconciled to their men of letters, he still felt angry towards the rest of the population. "You're an outsider here," the shrewd man he was talking to pointed out, "and while you see many abuses, you fail to see some of the hidden good that results even from those abuses. Among those writers there are some who aren't envious, and there are even some magi who are virtuous."

So, in the end, Babouc came to the conclusion that these large groups of men who – because of the violence of their disputes – seemed to deserve to be destroyed, were basically beneficial;

that each group of magi acted as a brake against the others; that though these groups were competing with each other, they were all preaching the same morality; that they were providing education for the people and were all subject to the law, in the same way as a tutor is in charge of the son of the house while the master of the house keeps an eye on the tutor. He got to know several of them and found that they were saintly souls. He even found that amongst those madmen who wanted to go to war against the Grand Lama there were some truly great men. He finally came to suspect that the morals of the citizens of Persepolis were like its buildings, some of which seemed to him frightful while others had filled him with admiration.

## Chapter X

HE SAID TO HIS FRIEND THE AUTHOR: "I can easily believe that those magi whom I'd thought to be so dangerous are, in fact, useful, particularly when a wise government ensures that they don't become indispensable, but at least you must admit that your young judges who've bought the right to be judges as soon as they're old enough to ride a horse are bound to appear ridiculous and presumptuous on the bench, and that it's grossly unjust. Surely it would be better for such honours to be offered, without payment, to those old jurists who've spent their whole lives weighing up the pros and cons of cases?"

"On your way to Persepolis," the man of letters replied, "you saw our army. You know that our young officers fight very well, although they bought their commissions. You may discover that our young judges are not so bad after all, despite the fact that they, too, bought their posts."

The following day, he took him to the High Court, where an important ruling was due to be delivered. Everybody knew about the case. All the old lawyers discussing it were uncertain in their views: they were quoting a hundred different precedents, none of which was particularly relevant to the central question; they were viewing the matter from all sides, not one of which threw much light on the matter. The judges made their decision long before the lawyers had managed to overcome their doubts. Their decision was almost unanimous: it was a good judgement because it was based on reason and insight; the lawyers had been misled because they were merely consulting their books.

Babouc concluded that abuses could often lead to good results. And that same day he also saw that the great wealth of banks could also have excellent effects: the Shah, finding himself in need of money, obtained through them more money in an hour than he could have raised in six months by ordinary means; he saw that those great clouds, swollen with dew from earth, could give back all that they had received in the form of rain. What's more, the children of these bourgeois upstarts, often better educated than those from older families, were sometimes a great deal more useful, for there's nothing to prevent anyone from being a good judge, a brave warrior or a clever diplomat when he's had a father who's done his sums right.

## Chapter XI

BABOUC WAS GRADUALLY BEGINNING to feel more kindly disposed towards the greed of the financiers, which, all things considered, was no worse than other people's and, moreover, was necessary. And he was finding excuses for those who were mad enough to ruin themselves in order to become judges or army officers, the sort of madness which can produce great judges or heroes. He felt forgiveness for envious men of letters, among whom there were many who were enlightening the world; he was becoming reconciled to ambitious, intriguing magi, amongst whom were to be found more virtues than petty vices; but he still felt many grievances, particularly in regard to the amorous goings-on of women, and he was worried and frightened at the thought of the havoc they must cause.

Being eager to explore the affairs of mankind at every level, he asked to be taken to meet a minister, and on the way was trembling at the thought of seeing a husband kill his faithless wife. On arriving at the statesman's rooms, he had to wait for two hours before being announced and another two before he was granted entry. During that time, he was promising himself that he would certainly advise Ituriel on how to deal with the minister and his insolent ushers. The anteroom was full of ladies of every rank, of magi of every sect, of judges, merchants, officers and pedants. They were all waiting to complain to the minister. Both the miser and the moneylender were saying: "There's no doubt that this man is mercilessly plundering the provinces"; there was a whimsical fellow accusing him of being eccentric; a hedonist said: "All he thinks about is his own pleasure"; an intrigant was happily predicting that he'd soon be overthrown by a plot and expressing the hope that he'd be replaced by someone younger.

Listening to their talk, Babouc couldn't help thinking: "He must be a very happy man: he's got all his enemies in one waiting room; he has the power to crush anyone who's envious of his position and he's got everyone who loathes him licking his boots."

Finally, he was shown in: he saw a little old man, bowed down by the weight of years and of his duties, but still lively and sharp-witted.

He took to Babouc and Babouc took to him. Their conversation became interesting. The Minister confessed that he was a very unhappy man: people thought he was rich and he was poor; that he was all-powerful and he was always meeting opposition; none of those he'd obliged had ever shown him any gratitude and in forty years of endless labour he'd never had a moment of consolation. Babouc was touched and thought that should Ituriel want to punish him all he needed to do was to force him to remain a minister.

## Chapter XII

WHILE HE WAS STILL TALKING to the minister, the beautiful girl with whom he'd dined came into the room; her eyes were full of pain and anger and she was weeping as she bitterly reproached the minister: he had refused to appoint her husband to a post for which not only his birth made him eminently suitable, but which he deserved by reason of the injuries he had suffered in his loyal services to the state. She was so forceful, pleaded so gracefully and argued so persuasively that she did not leave until she had ensured that her husband would be given the post. Babouc offered her his hand. "How is it possible, madam, that you have put yourself to so much trouble on behalf of a man of whom you're not fond and from whom you have so much to fear?"

"A man I'm not fond of?" she exclaimed. "'I have to inform you that he's my very best friend and there's nothing I wouldn't sacrifice for him – apart from my lover. And he'd do anything for me – except give up his mistress. I'll introduce you to her, she's a charming woman, very witty, a woman of excellent character. We're having dinner together this evening, with my little magus. Come and join our happy party."

The lady took Babouc back to her house. Her husband, who'd arrived quite disconsolate, was overjoyed and full of gratitude. He went round embracing everybody, his wife, his mistress, the little magus and Babouc. Joy and harmony and cheerfulness reigned supreme, everyone was witty and charming.

"Let me tell you," his lovely hostess said to Babouc, "that those women whom some people consider disreputable are almost always as good as a very decent man, and to convince you of this you must come and dine with me and the lovely Teona tomorrow. There may be a few ageing vestal virgins who are trying to tear her reputation to pieces, but she does more good than all of them put together and she'd never do any harm to anyone, even if it was in her own interest. Any advice she gives to her lover always comes from the heart, she thinks only of ways to further his interests. And he would be ashamed if she were to see him fail to take the opportunity to be of help to someone else, for there's nothing which encourages a man to be kind and decent more than knowing that a mistress whom you want to admire you is watching and judging the way you behave."

Babouc did not fail to go to the rendezvous. He found himself in a house given over to every possible pleasure and Teona was its queen. She knew how to address everyone in their own language and her natural wit put them all at their ease and encouraged them to be natural in their own way, and while she made little effort to be liked, everyone liked her. And, to add to all these charms, she was beautiful.

Although he was a Scythian and sent on a special mission by a genie, Babouc realized that if he were to stay on in Persepolis, Teona would make him forget Ituriel. He'd grown fond of this city, whose inhabitants were polite, gentle and kindly, even if they were also thoughtless, scandal-mongers and full of vanity. He was afraid that Ituriel might condemn Persepolis; he was even afraid of making his report on it.

He had an idea: he asked the best founder of the town to cast a statuette made out of every kind of metal, every sort of earth or clay, stones that were very precious or worth nothing at all. He took it and showed it to Ituriel.

"Would you smash this pretty little statue because it's not made purely of gold or diamonds?"

Ituriel took the hint; he decided not even to dream of reforming or punishing Persepolis and to let it continue to follow "the way of the world", for, as he said, "if not everything is good, everything is passable". So they let Persepolis go on as it was and Babouc was very far from complaining, unlike Jonah who was annoyed that they didn't destroy Nineveh*. But when you've spent three days in the belly of a whale, you're not quite as good-humoured as when you've been to the opera or seen a comedy, followed by a nice supper in pleasant company.

# Memnon

or

## Human Wisdom

O NE DAY, MEMNON HAD the odd idea of being perfectly wise. Most people have, sometime or other, let this mad idea flit through their head. Memnon said to himself: "Now, to be perfectly wise and, as a result, very happy, all I need to do is never to be passionate, which, as everybody knows, is quite simple. In the first place, I'll never fall in love with any woman; whenever I see a perfectly lovely girl, I'll say to myself: 'One day those cheeks will be covered in wrinkles, those lovely eyes will be red-rimmed, those lovely breasts will be sagging down, all flat, that lovely head will be bald. So I'll only need to look at her with the same eyes as I'll be seeing her then and that head will certainly no longer be turning mine. In the second place, I shall always be very frugal: however much I'm tempted by delicious wines, lovely food, the charm of pleasant company, I shall only have to think of the results of overindulgence, hangovers, a stomach upset, a dreadful headache, dizziness, ruining my health, wasting my time; so I'll eat only as much as I need; I'll be healthy, bright, clear-headed and cheerful. And it's all so easy that I shan't claim any credit for it.

"After which," Memnon went on, "I'll have to consider my financial situation. I have modest tastes, my assets are all safely on deposit with the tax collector's fund in Nineveh. I've got enough to live on, I'm independent, and that's the most important thing. I'll never have to go begging to anyone; I'll care for nobody and nobody will care for me. That's also very simple. I've got a few good friends and I intend to keep them, because there's nothing they'll want to get out of me. I'll never quarrel with them nor they with me. So there's no problem there either."

Having worked out his little programme for being wise, Memnon walked over to look out of his window and saw two women walking along together under the plane trees beside his house. One of them was old and didn't seem to be thinking of anything in particular; the other was young and pretty and seemed to have a lot on her mind; she was sighing and shedding tears, which were making her look even more charming. The wise Memnon was touched, not by her beauty – he was confident that he could resist any such temptation – but by her distress. He went down and spoke to the young Ninevite, hoping to console her with his wisdom. This lovely person told him with a heart-rendingly innocent air about all her troubles caused by her (quite fictitious) wicked uncle, who had craftily stolen some of her (equally fictitious) property. She said how frightened she was of his violence.

"You seem a man so full of sound advice," she said, "that if you would condescend to come home with me and examine my affairs, I'm sure you could rescue me from my predicament." Memnon had no hesitation in accompanying her to examine her situation and give her sound advice.

The lady in distress led him to a delicately scented room, politely offered him a seat on a wide sofa, where they sat facing each other with their legs crossed. With modestly lowered eyes, from which there dropped an occasional tear and which, when raised, always met those of Memnon, she told him her tale, full of emotion, which increased each time they exchanged glances. Memnon was taking her story greatly to heart and feeling all the time a growing desire to help such an honest and unhappy young woman. Without noticing it, in the heat of their conversation, they found themselves no longer sitting opposite each other. Their legs had, somehow or other, become uncrossed.

In the course of giving her sound advice, Memnon had come so close to her and was dispensing it with such tenderness that neither of them was capable of talking business any more and they could both no longer understand what was happening between them.

You will not be surprised to learn that, at this point, in comes the uncle, armed from head to foot, first of all saying that he'd kill both the wise Memnon and his niece, and eventually that he might be prepared to forgive and forget them both, in exchange for a considerable sum of money. Memnon handed over all the money he had on him. In those days, you were glad to get off so lightly; this was before they'd discovered America and damsels in distress were far less dangerous than they are today.

When Memnon returned home, ashamed and in great distress, he found a note from some old friends, inviting him to dine with them. "If I stay at home," thought Memnon, "I shall only go on worrying about that unfortunate mishap, I'll have lost my appetite and become ill. It'll be far better to go and have a frugal meal with some really good friends. Pleasant company like that will help me to forget how stupid I was." So he joined his friends who, finding him rather sad, plied him with wine, in order to cheer him up. Wine in moderation is good for body and soul, the wise Memnon thought – and promptly got drunk. After the meal, his friends suggested a game of cards. A quiet game of cards with friends is a nice way of spending an evening. He plays, loses every penny he's got on him and four times as much in promises. An argument arises, it becomes heated; one of these good friends flings a dice box at him, which blinds him in one eye. Wise Memnon is carried home drunk, incapacitated and short of an eye.

He sobered up a little and, as soon as his mind was a trifle clearer, he sent his valet to the tax collector's office to pick up the money he had deposited there, which he needed to pay his close friends. He was told that the fund had, that very morning, fraudulently, gone bankrupt; a hundred families would be seriously affected. Outraged, Memnon hurried round to the Court, with his eye in plaster, to petition the King to bring this bankrupt to justice. In a salon, he met a number of women, all gracefully attired in hooped skirts twenty-four feet in circumference. One of them, who knew him slightly, looked at him out of the corner of her eye and murmured: "How horrible!" Another one, who knew him better, said to him: "Good evening, Monsieur Memnon, how nice to meet you. And incidentally, Monsieur Memnon, why have you lost an eye?" She then went away without waiting for an answer.

Memnon retreated into a corner and waited for the opportunity to fling himself at his sovereign's feet. The moment came, Memnon prostrated himself to kiss the ground three times and handed his petition to the King. His Gracious Majesty accepted it most sympathetically and passed it to one of his satraps, so that he could give him a report on it. The satrap drew Memnon aside and said to him haughtily, with a sneer: "It really is very odd of you, you one-eyed little man, to approach the King on such a matter, instead of me, and even more bizarre to dare to ask for justice against such an honest bankrupt, who enjoys the honour of being a protégé of mine and who happens to be the nephew of my mistress's lady-in-waiting. If you want to keep the eye you still have, don't pursue this matter further, my dear fellow."

So, after having, that very morning, given up women, drinking too much, gambling, any kind of dispute and, above all, life at Court, Memnon had, by nightfall, been deceived and robbed by a lady, got drunk, gambled, had a quarrel and been to Court, where he'd been laughed at.

Stunned, bewildered and grief-stricken, he went away, sick at heart. He wanted to go into his house: he found bailiffs removing his furniture on the instructions of his creditors. As he was standing bemused under a plane tree, along came the lovely lady he'd given such good advice to that morning; she was with her uncle and when she saw Memnon's eye covered in a plaster she burst out laughing. Night fell and Memnon lay down on some straw beside his house. He became feverish, fell asleep and, in a dream, a celestial spirit appeared to him in a blaze of light. He had six wings but no head or tail or feet. He looked like nothing anyone had ever seen.

"Who are you?" asked Memnon.

"I'm your good genie," the spirit replied.

"Then give me back my eye, my property, my money, my health, my wisdom," said Memnon and explained how he had lost them all in a single day.

"Those are things that never happen in the world in which we live," said the spirit.

"And what world is that?" enquired Memnon sadly.

"The land in which I live," he replied, "is five hundred million leagues from the sun, in a little star next to Sirius, which you can see from here."

"What a lovely country!" exclaimed Memnon. "And so you really don't have any nasty women who deceive a poor man, good friends who relieve you of your money and your eye, no fraudulent bankrupts, no satraps making fun of you and denying you justice?"

"No," said the man from the star, "such unpleasant things never happen to us. We're never deceived by women because there aren't any, we never overindulge because we never eat, we don't have fraudulent bankrupts because we don't have any gold or silver or any money at all; we don't lose our eyes because our bodies are not made like yours and satraps are never unjust because, on our little star, we're all equal."

"But, my lord, how do you spend your time without food and women?"

"By keeping watch over other globes that have been entrusted to our care," said the celestial being. "I've come to console you."

"But why didn't you come last night, to prevent me from being so foolish?"

"I was with your elder brother in Assam," replied the spirit. "He's more to be pitied than you. His Most Gracious Majesty, the King of the Indies, at whose court he has the honour of serving, has, for some slight indiscretion, had both of his eyes put out and he is now lying shackled hand and foot in a dungeon."

"So what's the point of having a good angel," exclaimed Memnon with a sigh, "when one of two brothers has lost an eye and is sleeping on straw and the other is blind and in prison?"

"Your lot will change," replied the creature from the star, "and while it's true that you'll never have more than one eye, apart from that you'll be fairly happy, provided you never again have the silly idea of being perfectly wise."

"So that's impossible?" sighed Memnon.

"As impossible," replied the spirit, "as being perfectly clever, perfectly strong and powerful, perfectly happy. We ourselves are far from being any of those things. There does exist a globe where you can be all that, but in the hundred thousand millions of worlds scattered in space, everything is gradual: you are less wise, have less pleasure in the second one than in the first, and so it goes on until you reach the last one, in which everyone is completely mad."

"I'm very much afraid," commented Memnon, "that our little terraqueous globe may be precisely the little madhouse of the universe which you've just done me the honour of telling me about."

"Not quite," replied the good angel, "but you're getting rather close to it. There's a place for everything."

"But in that case," said Memnon, "certain poets, certain philosophers are very much mistaken when they say that all is well."

"No, they're quite right," said the philosopher from outer space, "if you take into account the organization of the whole universe."

"I'll believe that," poor Memnon replied, "when I've got my other eye back."

# Letter from a Turk

## about Fakirs and His Friend Bababec

W HEN I WAS IN THE CITY of Benares, on the banks of the Ganges, the former homeland of the Brahmins, I was eager to acquire knowledge. I could understand the language, more or less; I listened to what people around me were saying and I kept my eyes open for everything. I was lodging with my friend Omri, one of the most admirable men I ever knew: there was never a cross word between us on the subject of Muhammad and Brahma. We performed our ablutions side by side, shared the same lemon drink and ate the same rice; we were like two brothers.

One day we went together to the Gavani temple, where we saw several groups of fakirs. Some of them were janghis, that is to say meditative fakirs, and the others were disciples of the gymnosophists, who led a more active life. As you know, they speak a very learned language, the language of the earliest Brahmins, Sanskrit, in which is written the book called the Veda, surely the most ancient of all the books of Asia, even older than the Zend-Avesta.*

75

I passed a fakir who was reading a book. "O wretched infidel!" he cried. "You have made me forget how many vowels I had counted and now my soul will pass into the body of a hare instead of a parrot, as I had every reason to hope." To console him, I slipped him a rupee.

Unfortunately, a few yards farther on, I sneezed and woke up a fakir who was in a trance. "Where am I?" he said. "What a dreadful fall I've had. Now I've lost sight of the tip of my nose, which I need to watch in order to see the heavenly light. It's disappeared."

"If I was the one who made you lose sight of the end of your nose," I said, "let me give you a rupee to compensate for the harm I may have caused you, and please return to your celestial light."

Having thus discreetly extricated myself from this awkward situation, I went past some other gymnosophists; a number of them brought me some charming little nails to stick into my arms and thighs, in honour of Brahma. I bought the nails and used them to nail down my carpet.

Some fakirs were dancing about on their hands and others were flying around on a loose rope; some could move around only by hopping. Some were in chains, others were wearing a packsaddle; a few were hiding their heads in a bushel. Let me add that they were the nicest lot of people you'd ever wish to meet.

My friend Omri took me to the cell of the most famous fakir of all. He was called Bababec and was stark naked, with a large chain round his neck which weighed eighty pounds. He was sitting on a wooden chair, very nicely equipped with sharp little nails which were sticking into his buttocks, yet you might have thought he was sitting on a silk mattress. Lots of women used to come and consult him: he was a family oracle and he seemed to enjoy a tremendous reputation. I watched Omri having a long conversation with him.

"Do you think, Father, that after passing the test of the seven metamorphoses," he asked, "I can enter the abode of Brahma?"

"That depends," replied the fakir. "How do you spend your time?"

"I try to be a good citizen," he replied. "I'm a good husband, a good father, a good friend. I occasionally lend money to the rich, without charging any interest. I give money to the poor. I encourage my neighbours to live peaceably."

"Do you ever stick nails into your arse?" asked the fakir.

"Never, Reverend Father."

"That's unfortunate," said the fakir. "It's a pity, but you're certainly never going to get beyond the nineteenth heaven."

"What do you mean?" said Omri. "That's very good, I'll be quite content with that. What does it matter to me whether I get to the nineteenth or twentieth heaven, as long as I've done my duty during my pilgrimage on earth? I'll be made welcome at my final destination. Isn't it enough just to behave decently and then to be happy in the land of Brahma? What heaven do you intend to reach, Mister Bababec, with your chain and nails?"

"The thirty-fifth," replied Bababec.

"I think it's very curious of you," said Omri, "to claim to be ranked so much higher above me. It must be because you're excessively ambitious. You condemn people who want to be celebrated during their lifetime, so why do you want to be so grand in the next? And in any case, why do you claim you'll be better treated than I'll be? Let me tell you that I give more money to the poor in ten days than you spend in ten years on nails to stick in your backside. It's all very well for you to sit there all day stark-naked with a chain round your neck. How does that help your country? I have far more respect for a man who plants a tree than for all your fellow fakirs who squat watching their noses or wearing packsaddles to display what magnificent souls they have."

Having said which, he calmed down, told the fakir what a good man he was and persuaded him to give up his nails and his chain and come and live a decent life with him. They cleaned him up, rubbed him with scented oils and got him to dress properly. For a whole fortnight, he lived very sensibly and admitted that he felt a hundred times happier than he'd been before. But he was losing his prestige among the people; women had stopped coming to ask his advice. He left Omri and went back to his nails: he wanted to be a celebrity.

# Scarmentado's Travels

## Written by Himself

I WAS BORN IN 1600 IN CANDIA,* where my father was governor; I remember a mediocre poet called Iro, who was by no means mediocre in his truculence, who wrote a poor poem in praise of me, saying that I was directly descended from Minos, the son of Jupiter; when my real father fell into disgrace, he wrote another poem saying that I was descended from Pasiphaë and her lover, who, as you all know, was a bull and so produced a monster.* That Iro was an extremely nasty man and the most tiresome rogue on the island of Crete.

When I was fifteen, my father sent me to study in Rome. I arrived all eager to learn the truth about everything, because up till then I had been taught the exact opposite, as is the custom from China to the Alps. I'd been recommended to Cardinal Profondo, who was an odd man, one of the most terrifyingly learned men in the world. He was to teach me the categories of Aristotle and was ready to put me into the category of favourite boy; I had a narrow escape. I saw processions, exorcisms and a few molestations. It was said – mistakenly – that Signora Olimpia, a most prudent woman, was selling a lot of things as dispensations that weren't supposed to be sold. I was of an age when that sort of thing seemed very amusing. A very sweet-tempered young woman called Signora Fatelo took it into her head to fall in love with me. She was being wooed by the Reverend Father Aconiti and the Reverend Father Poignardini, young members of a religious order that no longer exists: she settled their disagreement by granting her favours to me, thereby putting me in danger of being excommunicated and poisoned as well. So I left: but I'd greatly enjoyed seeing St Peter's Basilica.

I went to France during the reign of Louis XIII, the Just King. The first thing I was asked was whether I'd like a small portion of the Maréchal d'Ancre for lunch; his flesh had been roasted by the people and was being sold off very cheaply to anyone who was interested.*

This country was being ravaged by civil war, sometimes to win a seat at the Council table, at other times because a couple of pages of a work were considered controversial. This fiery dispute, occasionally just smouldering, then bursting into flames, had been tearing this lovely country apart for the last sixty years. It was all about the freedom of the Gallican Church. "How sad!" I exclaimed. "What can have changed this people, so gentle by nature? They enjoy laughing and joking and they have the massacres of St Bartholomew.* Happy the day when they'll only be laughing and joking again!"

I crossed the Channel to England, where the same disputes were arousing the same fury. Holy Catholics had resolved, for the greater glory of the Church, to blow up, with gunpowder, the King, the royal family and the whole Parliament, and free England from these heretics. I was shown where the blessed Queen Mary, daughter of Henry VIII, had had more than five hundred of her subjects burnt to death. An Irish priest assured me that this was a very good act, first because those who'd been burnt were English and secondly because they didn't have any holy water and didn't believe in St Patrick. Above all, he was surprised that Queen Mary hadn't yet been canonized, but was hoping she would be, as soon as her nephew, who was also a cardinal, could find time to do it.

I went to Holland hoping to find less unrest among a more phlegmatic people. As I arrived in the Hague, they were cutting off the head of a venerable old man, the bald pate of the Prime Minister Barnevelt,* a man who had served his country supremely well. I felt greatly touched and asked what crime he'd committed: had he betrayed the State? "It was far worse than that," replied a preacher in a black robe. "He believed that a man can find salvation by good deeds as well as by faith. As you realize, if such beliefs were to prevail, any republic would be undermined and there must be strict laws to curb such dreadful doctrines." A most learned politician said to me with a sigh: "Alas, good times like these are doomed, they won't last; it's only by chance that this nation is so zealous since, basically, it tends towards the abominable dogma of tolerance and one day it will achieve that. It makes you shudder at the very thought."

As for me, before that disastrous time of toleration and forgiveness came I quickly got out of this country whose austerity was unrelieved by any charm. I took ship for Spain.

The Court was in Seville; the gallows had been set up; everything was bathed in abundance and joy at this loveliest season of the year. At the end of an avenue of orange and lemon trees, I could see a sort of immense arena surrounded by terraces swathed in costly fabrics. The King, the Queen, the Infantes and the Infantas were sitting under a superb canopy. Opposite this august family was another, higher throne. I said to one of my travelling companions: "Unless that throne is reserved for God, I can't understand why it's there." This indiscreet comment was overheard by a dour-faced Spaniard and was to cost me dearly. Meanwhile, as I was expecting to see a cavalcade or a bullfight, the Grand Inquisitor appeared, sat down on the other throne and blessed the King and the people.

An army of monks filed in, two by two, dressed in black, white and grey, barefooted or wearing sandals, bearded or beardless, with pointed cowls or cowl-less; they were followed by the executioner. Then, in the middle of the guards and nobles, you could see about forty people dressed in sackcloth, on which had been painted devils and flames. They were Jews who had refused to renounce Moses, Christians who had married their godmothers, who hadn't adored Our Lady of Atocha or who hadn't been prepared to hand over their cash to the Hieronymite friars. Lovely prayers were being very devoutly sung, after which all these guilty people were slowly burnt at the stake while the royal family seemed highly edified.

That evening, just as I was preparing to go to bed, I was visited by two members of the Inquisition of the Santa Hermandad. They tenderly embraced me and, without a word, led me into a very chilly prison cell; its furniture consisted of a mattress made of matting and a crucifix. There I remained for six weeks, at the end of which time the Reverend Father Inquisitor conveyed a request for me to come and talk with him. With true fatherly affection, he clasped me for a long while in his arms, saying how grieved he was to learn that I was so poorly accommodated, but that all the apartments in the house were occupied; he hoped that next time I should be made more comfortable. He then asked me, in a friendly manner, why I had been put there. I told the Reverend Father that it must have been for my sins.

"Well, my dear boy, for what sin? Please tell me very frankly."

Despite all my efforts, I was unable to think of any. He charitably tried to help me.

Finally, I remembered my indiscreet comment. They let me free, with a whipping and a fine of 30,000 ducats; they then took me to pay my respects to the Grand Inquisitor, who asked me very politely how I had enjoyed his little show. I told him that it had been delightful and rushed off to urge my travelling companions to leave this country, however lovely it was. They had had time to learn all the great deeds the Spaniards had done to further the cause of religion. They had read the memoirs of a famous bishop, according to which ten million infidels in America had been burnt at the stake or had their throats cut in order to convert them. I personally thought that the bishop had been exaggerating, but even if you halve that figure it's still a number to marvel at.

I hadn't yet lost the urge to travel. I'd been counting on finishing my European tour in Turkey and so we set off for there. I had the firm intention, from then on, never to express my opinion on any shows that we might be offered. "These Turks," I said to my fellow travellers, "are unbelievers who've never been baptized and as a result will be far more cruel than those reverend fathers, the Inquisitors. We must keep our mouths shut when we're with Muslims."

So off I went and was greatly puzzled to find that in Turkey there were many more Christian churches than in Candia. I even saw many groups of monks who were free to pray to the Virgin Mary and curse Muhammad, some in Greek, some in Latin, some in Armenian. "What good people the Turks are!" I exclaimed.

In Constantinople the Greek Christians and Latin Christians were deadly enemies, these slaves were persecuting each other like dogs fighting in the street and their masters have to beat them with their sticks to keep them apart. At that time the Grand Vizier was supporting the Greeks. The Greek Patriarch accused me of having had dinner with the Latin Patriarch and the Vizier's Council sentenced me to a hundred strokes of bastinado – which could be avoided by paying a fine of five hundred sequins. The next day, the Grand Vizier was strangled and the day after he was replaced by a vizier who supported the Latin Christians – he wasn't strangled until a month later, so he had time to fine me the same amount for having had dinner with the Greek Patriarch. I thus found myself in the sad predicament of being unable to frequent either the Greek or the Latin Christian churches. To console myself, I hired the services of an extremely beautiful Circassian who in private concourse was the most tender of women and in a mosque the most devout. One night, carried away by the delights of love, she cried out: "Allah! Illah! Allah!", which, for the Turks, are holy words. I took them to be words of love and exclaimed, equally tenderly: "Allah! Illah! Allah!"

"Ah!" she cried. "Allah be praised; through his mercy you've become a Turk!"

I told her that I was thanking God for giving me such strength and because I was so happy. Next morning the imam came to circumcise me and, when I proved difficult to persuade, the local district magistrate, a loyal man, offered to impale me. Saving my foreskin and my backside cost me a thousand sequins. I quickly left for Persia, determined in future never to attend either a Greek or a Latin mass and never to exclaim: "Allah! Illah! Allah!" while enjoying a rendezvous.

On arriving in Isfahan, I was asked whether I supported black sheep or white sheep. I replied that I couldn't care less, as long as the meat was tender. Here I must explain that at that time the Persians were still divided into two factions, the Black and the White Sheep. They thought that I was making fun of both sects, and when I arrived at the city gates I was faced by a very awkward problem. I managed to solve it only by once again handing over quite a large number of sequins in order to appease the sheep.

So I moved on all the way to China with an interpreter who assured me that it was indeed the country where you could live freely and happily. It had just been conquered by the Tartars, after they had put the whole country to fire and sword, and the reverend Jesuit fathers on the one hand and the reverend Dominican fathers on the other were both claiming that they were winning souls to God without anyone noticing. You've never met anybody keener to convert somebody else and then taking it in turns to persecute each other. They were sending tome after tome of slander back to Rome, calling each other infidels who were corruptly converting souls. Above all they were engaged in a bitter quarrel as to the proper way to bow: the Jesuits wanted the Chinese to show their respect towards their parents by bowing in the Chinese way, while the Dominicans wanted it done in the Roman way. It so happened that the Jesuits suspected me of being a Dominican and I was denounced to the Tartar Majesty as a papist spy. The Supreme Council made a request to the Chief Mandarin, who ordered a sergeant, who instructed four local sbirri to arrest me and tie me up, with due ceremony. After making a hundred and forty kowtows, I was led up to His Majesty, who enquired whether I was spying for the Pope and whether it was true that the aforementioned Prince was coming, in person, to dethrone him. I replied that the Pope was a seventy-year-old priest who lived some four thousand miles or so from His August Sino-Tartar Majesty; that his army consisted of about two thousand men who, when mounting guard, took good care to stay in the shade of a parasol; that he never dethroned anyone; and that His Sacred Majesty could sleep in peace.

This adventure was the least disastrous of all my travels. I was sent to Macao, where I took ship for Europe. The ship had to be refitted on the shores of Golconda, and I took the opportunity to visit the court of the mighty Aurangzeb,* the tale of whose marvellous exploits was spreading far and wide. At that time, he was in Delhi. I was rewarded by seeing him during the ceremony, accompanied with great pomp, when he received the celestial gift sent to him by the sheriff of Mecca. It was the broom with which they had swept the floor of the shrine of Kaaba, the house of Allah, symbolizing the cleansing of the soul of all its filth. Aurangzeb hardly seemed to need it, since he was the most pious man in the whole of Hindustan, though it's true that he'd cut the throat of one of his sons and poisoned his own father. And twenty Hindu rajas and an equal number of Muslim umrahs had also been tortured to death; all this was quite irrelevant: he was devout and thus praised by all. Only His Sacred Majesty, Moulay Ismail, His Most Serene Highness the Sultan of Morocco, was worthy to be compared to him: he cut off people's heads every Friday after prayers.

I lay low and said nothing; I had learnt that lesson from my travels and I felt that it wasn't up to me to decide between the virtues of these two divine sovereigns. A young Frenchman with whom I was sharing lodgings failed, I must confess, to show due respect to the Emperor of the Indians and the Emperor of Morocco. He took it into his head to say, very indiscreetly, that in Europe there were extremely pious monarchs who governed their countries well and even went to church without cutting off their subjects' heads and killing their fathers and brothers. Our interpreter passed on the impious comments of this young man. Having learnt by experience, I quickly had our camels saddled and we both left. I later learnt that officers of the great Aurangzeb had come to get us but found only the interpreter. He was publicly executed and the courtiers all admitted that, in all honesty, he fully deserved his fate.

To enjoy every delight that our world has to offer, I still had to see what Africa was like. And I certainly did... My ship was captured by African pirates. Our skipper protested violently and demanded to know why they were violating the accepted laws of the sea in this way. The black captain retorted: "You have long noses, ours are squat, your skin is the colour of ashes, ours is the colour of ebony. The result of this is that the sacred laws of nature decree that we must always be enemies. You buy us in slave markets on the coast of Guinea and use us as beasts of burden, making us work on various tasks, all equally ridiculous and painful; we're whipped, forced to dig in the mountains to extract a yellow sort of rock which in itself has absolutely no value at all and is far less appealing than a good Spanish onion – I believe you call it gold?

And so when we come across you and we're stronger than you are, we make you our slaves, forcing you to plough our fields, or else we'll cut off your nose and ears."

Such a well-argued case was unanswerable. I was sent to plough the fields of an old black woman, thereby saving my nose and my ears. A year later, I was ransomed. I had seen all that was beautiful and good and admirable on earth. I resolved never again to worship anything but my own household gods. I married a local girl, she made me a cuckold and I realized that it was the most peaceful way of life in the world.

# Consolation for Two

O NE DAY THE GREAT PHILOSOPHER Citophile said to a grief-stricken woman, who had every reason to be grieving:

"Dear lady, the Queen of England, the daughter of our great King Henry IV, was as unhappy as you. Driven out of her kingdom, she nearly perished in a storm at sea. She saw her royal husband, Charles I, beheaded on the scaffold."*

"I'm most sorry for her," said the lady and began to weep over her own misfortunes.

"And don't forget Mary Stuart," said Citophile. "She was honourably in love with a nice man, a musician with a very fine bass voice. Her husband killed her musician before her own eyes and, later on, her good friend and half-sister Elizabeth, the one who said she was a virgin queen, had her head cut off after keeping her in prison for eighteen years."*

"That was very cruel of her," replied the lady and remained plunged in grief.

The philosopher was still determined to console her.

"You may perhaps have heard of the lovely Joanna of Naples,* who was kidnapped and strangled?"

"I vaguely remember her," replied the lady, still disconsolate.

"I must tell you," pursued the consoling philosopher, "about a sovereign queen who, in my own day, was dethroned and died on a desert island."

"I know all about that," replied the lady.

"Well then, let me tell you what happened to another great princess to whom I was teaching philosophy. Like all great and beautiful princesses, she had a lover. Her father came into her room and caught the lover by surprise; his face was flushed, his eyes were sparkling like carbuncles. Her father took such a dislike to the young lover that he gave him the most enormous slap in the face; never before had anyone seen such a slap in that part of the world. The lover picked some fire tongs and struck his father-in-law on the head so hard that he barely survived and still bears the scar. The distraught princess leapt out of the window and dislocated her foot, as a result of which she now has a perceptible limp, though otherwise she still has a superb figure. Her lover was condemned to death for cracking the skull of such a very noble prince. You can imagine the state of mind of the princess as they took her lover away to be executed. I used to visit her every so often while she was being held in prison: she could talk of nothing else but her dreadful misfortune."

"Then why mayn't I think about mine?" enquired the lady.

"Because you mustn't think about it," replied the philosopher, "and since so many great ladies have endured such misfortune, it's wrong of you to be so despairing. Just think of Niobe, think of Hecuba."*

"Ah, if I'd lived in those days," said the lady, "or in the days of so many lovely princesses, and if, to console them, you'd told them of my sorrows, would they have listened to you?"

The very next day, the philosopher lost his only son and he nearly died of grief. The lady drew up a list of all the kings whose children had been killed and showed it to the philosopher, who, after reading it, said it was very accurate... and continued to mourn as much as before.

Three months later, they met again and were amazed to discover that they were both very cheerful. So together they had a fine statue erected on the base of which was engraved:

TO TIME, THE GREAT HEALER.

# Story of a Good Brahmin

I N THE COURSE OF MY TRAVELS I met an old Brahmin, a very wise, erudite and intelligent man; what's more, he was rich and that made him even wiser, because, as he had everything, he didn't need to lie to anyone. His family was very well cared for by his three beautiful wives and, when he was not enjoying their company, he would spend his time philosophizing.

Close by his house, which was lovely, well furnished and set in charming gardens, there lived an old Hindu woman, bigoted, idiotic and rather poor.

One day he said to me: "I wish I'd never been born." I asked him why and he replied: "I've been studying now for forty years and those years were all wasted. I teach other people but I don't know anything, and that makes me feel so humiliated and disgusted with myself that I find life unbearable. I've been born and I live in time and I've no idea what Time really is; I exist at a point between two eternities, as men say, and I've no idea of eternity; I'm made of matter; I think and I've never been able to learn what produces thought; I don't know if my power of understanding is merely a function, like walking or digesting, and whether I think with my head in the same way as I grasp something with my hands. Not only am I ignorant of the workings of my brain, I'm uncertain of how I move my limbs; I don't know why I exist, yet every day people are asking questions on all these matters and I have to give them an answer; I talk a great deal, although I've nothing worth saying, and then I feel embarrassed, ashamed of what I've said. And it's even worse when I'm asked whether it was Vishnu who was produced by Brahma or if they are both eternal. May God be my witness, I really don't know a thing about it, which becomes obvious from the way I answer. People say to me: 'O Reverend Father, please tell me how it is that the whole world is full of evil,' and I'm just as baffled as those who are questioning me: I sometimes reply that everything in the world is for the best, and then those who have been mutilated in a war don't believe what I've told them any more than I do myself. I retreat into my house, weighed down by my desire to know and by my ignorance. I read our revered old books and they leave me even more in the dark. I talk with my companions: some tell me that life must be enjoyed and you mustn't care about other people, others think that they know something and lose their way in a maze of wild ideas. All this just increases my feeling of unhappiness. Sometimes, when I reflect that after all my searching, I don't know where I come from, what I am, where I'm going, what will become of me, I feel close to despair."

I felt sorry for this good man, for I knew him to be the most reasonable and most sincere of men, and I realized that the more enlightened his mind and the more sensitive his heart became, the unhappier he grew.

That same day, I saw the old woman who lived nearby and I asked her if she ever felt miserable, seeing that she knew nothing about the state of her soul. She didn't even understand what I meant; she'd never in her whole life given a single thought to these things that were tormenting the old Brahmin; she believed wholeheartedly in the metamorphoses of Vishnu and she considered herself the happiest woman in the world, as long as she could, now and then, have some water from the Ganges to wash in.

I was struck by this old woman's happiness and went back to my philosopher and said: "Aren't you ashamed at being so miserable when, practically on your doorstep, you have an old automaton who is perfectly content to live without ever thinking about anything at all?"

"You're perfectly right," he replied, "I've told myself time and again that if I were as stupid as my neighbour I'd be happy, and yet I wouldn't enjoy that sort of happiness."

The Brahmin's reply made a greater impression on me than anything I'd ever heard. I examined myself and realized that I wouldn't, in fact, have liked to be happy if it required me to be an idiot.

I put the question to some philosophers; they agreed with me. "All the same," I said, "there's a tremendous contradiction in that way of thinking; after all, what are we talking about? Being happy: what's the importance of being intelligent or being stupid?

Moreover, those people who are content with their lot are quite sure they're happy, whereas those who go around thinking aren't sure that they're thinking properly. So it's obvious that we ought to choose not to have common sense, if having it contributes to making us feel unhappy."

Everyone shared my view, yet I couldn't find a single person prepared to accept the option of becoming a moron in order to be happy. From which I drew the conclusion that, even if we think it's important to be happy, we think it even more important not to be stupid.

All the same, after due consideration, it does seem that it's really mad to prefer reason to happiness. So how can this contradiction be resolved? This isn't a matter to be lightly dismissed: it still requires a great deal of discussion.

# Jeannot and Colin

A NUMBER OF RELIABLE PERSONS claim to have seen Jeannot and Colin at school in Issoire, in the Auvergne; Issoire is famous throughout the universe for this school and its cooking pots. Jeannot was the son of a very well-known muleteer, while Colin owed his existence to an honest, worthy farmer in the neighbourhood who had four mules to plough his land and, after he'd paid all his various rates and taxes – salt tax, poll tax, tithe etc. etc. – was not vastly wealthy at the end of the year.

Jeannot and Colin were pleasant-looking youngsters, by Auvergne standards, and were very fond of each other and took little liberties with each other that we always have pleasure in recalling when we meet again later in life. Just when their time at school was coming to an end, a tailor came and gave Jeannot a velvet frock coat – in three colours! – and a very smart jacket – from Lyon – together with a letter addressed to Monsieur de la Jeannotière. Colin admired the frock coat and didn't feel envious, but Jeannot assumed a superior air that made Colin feel unhappy. From that time on, Jeannot stopped studying, kept looking at himself in the mirror and looked down on everybody. A short while later, a valet arrived in a post-chaise, with a second letter addressed to the Marquis de la Jeannotière: his father was ordering his son to come to Paris. Jeannot got into the post-chaise and, with a somewhat aristocratically patronizing smile, offered Colin his hand to shake, making Colin realize that he was a nonentity and shed a tear. Jeannot left, pompous and glorious.

Readers who like to learn something from what they read will now be told that Monsieur Jeannot Senior had rather rapidly acquired an immense fortune through his business affairs. Are you asking me how one manages to do that? It's by being lucky. Monsieur Jeannot was well built, his wife was too and she still looked youthful. They went to Paris for a lawsuit which was ruining them, when Lady Luck, who makes men rise and fall as the whim takes her, brought them into contact with an enterprising man in charge of military hospitals, a very talented individual who could boast of having succeeded in killing more soldiers in one year than had been killed by gunfire in ten. The wife took to Jeannot; the husband took to his wife. Jeannot soon became a partner in the hospital business; then he went into other businesses. As soon as you're in the flow, all you have to do is to let yourself float along; you'll have no trouble at all in earning millions and millions. Those mischief-makers on the river bank goggle in amazement as they see you glide by in full sail; they don't know how you've managed it, they envy you without exactly knowing why and write pamphlets attacking you which you don't bother to read. And this is what happened to Jeannot Senior, soon to become Monsieur de la Jeannotière, and, six months after buying the title, he sent for his son Jeannot (soon to become the Marquis de la Jeannotière) to leave school and come to Paris and go into high society.

Still very fond of Jeannot, Colin wrote to congratulate his old school friend. The little marquis didn't reply. Colin was deeply hurt.

First of all, Jeannot's father and mother provided him with a tutor: this tutor looked rather grand, was very ignorant and incapable of teaching his pupil anything. The father wanted his son to learn Latin, his mother was against it, so they decided to ask the opinion of an author, celebrated at the time for writing pleasant little stories. They asked him to dinner. The master of the house began by saying: "As you know Latin and mix in Court circles—"

"I know Latin?" replied the witty writer. "I don't know a word of Latin, and a good job too. It's perfectly obvious that you speak French better when you don't waste your time and effort on foreign languages and stick to your own. Look at our ladies: they express themselves far more agreeably than men and their letters are infinitely more graceful. And they owe their superiority over men purely to the fact that they don't know any Latin."

"So you see I was right," said Madame de la Jeannotière. "I want my son to be a wit and make his mark in society, and it's quite obvious that if he knew Latin, he'd be sunk. May I ask if there's anyone who writes comedies or operas in Latin? If you're involved in a lawsuit, do you need to speak Latin? Does anyone make love in Latin?"

Dazzled by such logic, her husband also consigned Latin to oblivion, and it was decided that the young marquis wouldn't waste his time on Cicero, Horace or Virgil. "But what is he to learn, then? After all, he's got to know something; couldn't he be taught a bit of geography?"

"What's the good of that?" asked the tutor. "When the marquis goes to inspect his estates, won't the postilions know the way? They'll certainly not get lost. You don't need a quadrant to make a journey and you can go from Paris to Auvergne very comfortably without needing to know what latitude you're in."

"Of course," replied the father. "But I have heard of a very fine science called, I believe, astronomy."

"Pitiful!" retorted the tutor. "When we're on earth, do we go by the stars? Will the young marquis have to work himself to death calculating that there'll be an eclipse when he'll be able to find out any time he wants to in his almanac, as well as all the moveable feasts, the quarters of the moon and the age of every European princess?"

Madame de la Jeannotière wholeheartedly agreed with the tutor and the young marquis was highly delighted. His father remained undecided.

"Then what is my son to learn?" he enquired.

"He must learn to be likeable," advised the friend whom they consulted. "If he can make other people like him, that's all he needs to know. And it's an art which he can learn from his mother, without causing any difficulty for either of them."

On hearing this, the mother embraced this likeable, ignorant friend.

"You're the cleverest man in the world. My son shall be brought up by nobody else but you, though I think it might not be a bad idea for him to know a little history."

"What good will that be to him? Certainly, it's useful and interesting to know something about what's happening around you, but as one of our wits recently remarked, all ancient history only consists of hackneyed fables, and as for modern times, it's sheer chaos and incomprehensible. And what's the point of your son knowing that Charlemagne nominated twelve French peers and that his successor had a stammer?"

"It couldn't have been better put!" exclaimed the tutor. "A child's mind becomes stifled under a pile of useless knowledge. But in my opinion, of all the sciences the most absurd and the most liable to stifle any sort of genius is geometry. This ridiculous science deals with surfaces, lines and points that don't exist in nature. A geometrician will see a hundred thousand curved lines passing between a circle and a straight line whereas in reality not even a wisp of straw could get through. The truth is that geometry is just a bad joke."

The Jeannotières were in complete agreement, though they didn't quite understand what the tutor was talking about.

"A lord like the young marquis," he continued, "mustn't lumber his mind with such pointless things. If, one day, he ever wants an eminent geometrician to survey his land, he'll give him the money to do all the measuring. If he wants to unravel his noble ancestry, which certainly goes back to a most remote past, he'll send for a learned Benedictine. It's the same for all the arts. A young, well-born lord isn't a painter or a musician or an architect or a sculptor, but he's very glad to be able to support and encourage all those arts by his magnanimity. There's no doubt that it's better to sponsor them than to practise them: all that the marquis needs is to have good taste; it's the artist's job to do the work for him, and that's why it's very right and proper that ladies and gentlemen of quality – *by which term I mean the very rich* – know everything without ever having learnt anything, because, at the end of the day, they do indeed know how to pass judgement on all the things they've ordered – and are paying for."

At this point the amiable ignoramus spoke up:

"You've certainly noticed that man's principal aim in life is to make his way successfully in society. And frankly, can he achieve that by being very learned? In the best society, has it ever occurred to anyone to talk about geometry? Is any gentleman ever asked what star will be appearing in the sky at the same time as the sun? At dinner parties, does anyone ever enquire if Chlodio the Longhair* crossed the Rhine?"

"Of course not!" exclaimed the Marquise de la Jeannotière, whose physical attractions had, at times, given her access to high society, "and my dear son must not allow his outstanding gifts to be ruined by all that rubbish. But what can we teach him then?

As my husband pointed out, it's important for him to be able to be brilliant in something. I remember hearing an *abbé* say that the most agreeable science was something I've forgotten the name of – it began with an H."

"An H, madam? Didn't we agree that history was useless?"

"Yes, I know, though it did end in a Y."

"Ah, I have it, madam! It's heraldry. And it is indeed a very profound subject, but it's gone out of fashion ever since they stopped putting coats of arms on coach doors. But it's certainly most useful in any really civilized society. What's more, studying heraldry would offer an infinitely wide field. But these days, even barbers have got their coats of arms and, as you know, once something becomes common, it ceases to be quite so respectable."

In the end, after weighing up the pros and cons of various sciences, they decided that the young marquis should be taught dancing. But Nature, all-powerful Nature, had given him one skill which turned out to be a tremendous success: he was an excellent singer of vaudeville ditties. This supreme gift, together with his youthful charm, led people to see him as a young man of the highest promise. Women adored him and, as his head was full of songs, he wrote some for his mistresses. He borrowed bits of his 'Bacchus and Love' from one vaudeville, of 'Night and Day' from another and of 'Charms and Alarms' from a third. But as he found his lines always either two or three feet too long or too short, he paid a hack to correct them, twenty gold louis per song and they were put into the *Annual Literary Review*, together with the work of some rather better-known versifiers.

So the Marquise de la Jeannotière came to think that her son was a dashing young wit and invited all the dashing young wits of Paris to dinner. This all quickly went to the young man's head: he learnt the art of saying things that he himself didn't understand and honed to perfection the habit of not being any good at anything at all. Seeing how bright he was, his father greatly regretted not having had him learn Latin, because then he'd have been able to buy him some high office in the legal profession. His mother, who had more elevated ambitions, tried to find a regiment for him. Meanwhile he had love affairs and, as love sometimes costs more than a regiment, he got through a lot of money, while his parents were squandering even more in their effort to live on a grand scale.

A neighbour of theirs, a young widow and a lady of quality, though not very well off, decided that she would be happy to take over the task of safeguarding the de la Jeannotières' wealth and getting it into her own hands by marrying the young marquis. She enticed him into her apartment, let him make love to her, hinted that she liked his company, led him on inch by inch, bewitched him and had no difficulty in getting him under her thumb. She alternated flattery with advice and became his father's and mother's best friend. An old lady, another neighbour, suggested marriage. Dazzled by such a brilliant match, the parents joyfully accepted the suggestion: they were giving their son to a close friend. The young marquis was going to marry the woman he adored and who loved him; their friends congratulated him; the marriage settlement was drawn up; people started working on the wedding dress and the wedding songs.

One morning, filled with thoughts of love and the friendship and respect that he would enjoy when she became his wife, he was kneeling at the feet of his charming bride and having a lively, tender conversation with her, making plans for their wonderful future together, when one of his mother's servants came in, looking very alarmed.

"Something very unexpected has happened," he said. "Bailiffs have come to take away all the contents of your parents' house. Everything's been seized by their creditors. They're talking about arresting someone, so I'm going to be quick and make sure I get the wages I'm owed."

"What on earth are you talking about?" said the young marquis. "I must go and see what's causing all this fuss."

"Yes, indeed," said the young widow. "Go and punish these scoundrels straight away."

He rushed round to his house, discovered that his father was already in jail and all the servants had disappeared, taking with them everything they could lay hands on. His mother was all alone, with no one to help or console her. She was crying bitterly; she'd been left with nothing but memories of her wealth, of her beauty, her mistakes and her wild extravagance.

In the end, after her son had spent a long time weeping at his mother's side, he said:

"We mustn't despair. That young widow is desperately in love with me; she's rich and generous. I can vouch for that and I'll go and see her at once and bring her back with me to console you."

So he goes back to his bride and finds her in private conversation with a very personable young officer.

"So it's you, Monsieur de la Jeannotière. What brings you back here? How can anyone desert his mother like that? Go back to that poor woman at once, tell her that I'm still very fond of her, that I need a chambermaid and will be very happy to take her on."

"Well, my lad," said the officer, "you look well set up. If you want to join my company, I'll be glad to find you a decent job."

The young marquis was stupefied and completely outraged. He went to consult his former tutor, told him of his woes and asked what he should do.

"Do what I did: become a tutor."

"But I'm afraid I don't know anything that I could teach; you never taught me anything," he sobbed. "You're the main reason for this dreadful situation I'm in."

"Why not write novels?" asked a witty courtier. "In Paris that's a very handy way of making money."

More desperate than ever, the young marquis hurried round to see his mother's confessor, a very prominent Theatine who exclusively advised ladies with the highest connections. As soon as he saw the young marquis, he hurried to greet him.

"Goodness me, what's happened to your coach? And how is the excellent marquise, your dear mother?"

The miserable young man told him of the disaster which had overtaken his family. As he listened, the confessor's manner grew noticeably more serious, cooler and loftier.

"This is God's will, my son; wealth serves only to corrupt the heart. Is your mother, by the grace of God in His wisdom, reduced to utter destitution?"

"Yes, Reverend Father."

"Excellent! He has ensured her salvation."

"But mightn't there be, meanwhile, any chance of finding help in this world?"

"Goodbye, my son. I can see a lady from the Court waiting to speak to me."

The young marquis was close to collapse. He met more or less the same reception from all his friends and, in the course of half a day, learnt more about society than ever before.

In the depths of despair, he saw a sort of old-fashioned wheelchair approaching; this odd type of tipcart had been fitted with a hood and leather curtains and was followed by four enormous, heavily laden wagons. It was being driven by a rather shabbily dressed young man; he had a fresh, very friendly and cheerful-looking round face. His little wife, a rather pleasant-looking young brunette with somewhat coarse features, was being jolted about beside him. The cart bore not the slightest resemblance to the chariot of some dashing young dandy and the couple had ample time to look at the young marquis standing there motionless and plunged in grief.

"My goodness!" exclaimed the driver of the cart. "I think that's Jeannot!"

Hearing his name, the young marquis looks up. The cart stops – "Yes, it's Jeannot!" – and the rotund little man jumps out and dashes across to embrace his old school friend.

Seeing Colin, Jeannot was covered in shame; tears came into his eyes.

"You deserted me," said Colin, "but I shall never desert you. I like you, even if you are a lord."

Jeannot was deeply touched and embarrassed, and when he began to tell him something of what had happened, he started sobbing.

"Come into the inn where we're staying and tell me everything," said Colin. "Give my little wife a kiss and let's have dinner together."

The three set off, followed by all the baggage.

"What is all this that you've got in there? Is it yours?" asked Jeannot.

"Yes, all mine and my wife's. We've just come from our place in the country. I run a big tin and copper factory. My wife's the daughter of a rich businessman who sells all sorts of things used by everybody, rich or poor. We work hard. God's been kind to us. We haven't moved up in society, we're just happy and would like to help our friend Jeannot. Stop being a marquis; all the grandees in this world aren't worth a good friend. You'll come back home with us. I'll teach you the trade; it's not all that difficult. I'll make you my partner and we'll go on living happily in the place where we were born."

Completely bewildered, Jeannot didn't know whether to be happy or sad. He was full of love and shame.

"All my fine friends have let me down," he said to himself, "and Colin, whom I looked down on, is the only one to come to my help. What a lesson for me!"

Colin's kindness sparked a change of heart in Jeannot; his basic good nature hadn't been completely destroyed.

"We'll take care of your mother," said Colin, "and as for your dear old dad, I know a thing or two about business matters; as soon as his creditors realize that he hasn't a bean, they'll be prepared to settle for very little. I'll see to everything."

And so he did, and Jeannot's father was soon set free. Jeannot came back to his home town and his parents went back to their old jobs. Jeannot married one of Colin's sisters, who took after her brother and made him very happy.

So Jeannot Senior, his wife Jeannotte and Jeannot Junior realized that vanity doesn't bring happiness.

# Wives, Submit Yourselves unto Your Own Husbands

THE WIFE OF MARSHAL DE GRANCEY* was a very commanding woman and, indeed, did possess many fine qualities. She prided herself on her self-respect, on never doing anything she would privately be ashamed of; she would never demean herself to tell a lie and, rather than prevaricate, she would be prepared to admit the truth, even if that might prove dangerous; she said that prevarication was always cowardly. In the course of her life, she had performed many generous actions, but when people praised her for them, she felt that they were being condescending and would say: "So you think I found that difficult to do?" Her friends loved her, her lovers adored her and she was respected by her husband.

She lived a self-indulgent life for some forty years, in that cycle of entertainments which are of such serious concern for women; the only things she ever read were the letters people wrote her; she was interested only in the news of the day, the foolish behaviour of those around her and her own love affairs. Finally, seeing that she had reached the age when they say lovely women who are also intelligent should move on to something different, she decided to take up reading. She began with the tragedies of Racine and was surprised to discover that she enjoyed them more than when she had seen them on the stage; her taste was expanding and she realized that this man had never said anything that wasn't true and interesting, and that everything had been put exactly in its right place, that he was simple, noble, with nothing declamatory or forced, no attempt to be clever; that his plots as well as his thoughts were all based on nature; as she read she could see a reflection of her own feelings, the picture of her own life.

They gave her Montaigne to read. She was charmed by this man who chatted with her and had doubts about everything. Next they gave her Plutarch's *Lives of Great Men*, and she enquired why he hadn't written some *Lives of Great Women*.

One day when the Abbé de Châteauneuf, my godfather, called on her, he noticed that her face was flushed with anger and enquired what was wrong.

"I've just picked up a book which happened to be lying about in my study – I think it was a collection of letters and I read a few words, saying something like: 'Wives, you must submit to your husbands'. I just tossed it onto the floor!"

"But, my dear lady, don't you know that that was one of the Epistles of St Paul?"

"I don't care who wrote them – he must have been a very ill-bred man. My husband, the Marshal, never said or wrote anything like that to me. I suspect that your St Paul must have been a very difficult man to get on with. Was he married?"

"Yes, madam."

"His wife must have been a very long-suffering woman. If I'd had a husband like that, I'd have soon shown him what's what! *Submit to your own husbands*, indeed! If he'd just said: be gentle, indulgent, understanding, thrifty, I'd have recognized that, at least, he was well bred. But why *submit*, if you please? When I married Grancey, we promised to be faithful to each other; well, I didn't quite manage to keep my word and neither did he. But neither of us ever promised to obey. Are we slaves? Isn't it enough that, after marrying you, he has the right to give you an illness that lasts for nine months... and may prove fatal? Isn't it enough that I gave birth – extremely painfully – to a child who, once he comes of age, will be able to take me to court? Isn't it enough that every month an extremely unpleasant event occurs, quite unseemly for a lady of quality? And moreover, when one of those dozen events fails to take place, I'm placed in a situation which may lead to my death? And on top of all that, I'm supposed to submit to him as well! I'm certain Nature never said anything like that: we were merely given organs different from men's, but while that may make us dependent on each other, Nature never claimed that this would be a form of slavery. I do remember Molière writing:

Power belongs to him who can grow a beard*

"But that's a very odd reason for me to accept a master. Just because a man's chin is covered in a nasty, rough stubble and I was born with a chin already shaven, am I supposed to be his most humble servant? I admit that men have stronger muscles than ours and that they can deliver a more powerful punch. And to tell you the truth, I'm afraid that's the basic reason for their claiming to be superior. But they also claim to have a more methodical brain than ours, and that's why they boast of being more capable of governing; however, I can show them queens who were just as good as kings. People were talking to me yesterday about a German princess called Catherine* who gets up at five every morning to look after the welfare of her subjects, who concerns herself with everything, deals with all her correspondence herself, supports the arts and who's as kind as she's enlightened. And she's as brave as she is clever, for she hasn't been brought up in a convent, where they teach us what things we mustn't know and fail to teach us the things we need to know. For my part, if I were in charge of governing a state, I think I'd be bold enough to model myself on her."

Being a very polite man, the Abbé de Châteauneuf took good care not to contradict the lady.

"Talking of which," she went on, "is it true that Muhammad had such a low opinion of women that he claimed that we aren't entitled to go to heaven and wouldn't be allowed beyond the entrance?"

"If that were the case," replied the *abbé*, "it would be men who would be in charge at the door. But console yourself, madam, there's not a single word of truth in what is said about Islam among us. Our wretched ignorant monks were misleading us, as my brother has explained – he spent twelve years as an ambassador in Constantinople."

"What? Isn't it true that, in order to enlist men's support, Muhammad invented the idea that they should be allowed to have a large number of wives? Isn't it true that in Turkey women are nothing better than slaves and we're not even allowed to pray in mosques?"

"Completely untrue, madam. Far from preaching polygamy, he repressed and restricted it. You'll recall that our own wise Solomon owned seven hundred wives; Muhammad reduced that to just four. Ladies will go to heaven just like men and no doubt they'll make love there, though in a different sort of way from here, because, as you know, in this world people have a very imperfect idea of love."

"Yes, I'm afraid that's the case," replied Madame de Grancey. "Men aren't really much good. But do tell me, did your Muhammad really ordain that women should submit to their husbands?"

"No, madam, that's not in the Koran."

"Then why are they slaves in Turkey?"

"They're not slaves at all. They can own property, make their own wills, ask for a divorce, in the appropriate circumstances; they go to the mosque at their own times – and to their rendezvous at other times; you see them in the street with their veils covering their noses, just as you yourself used to wear a mask a few years ago. It's true that you won't see them at the opera or the theatre, they don't exist there. Can you have any doubt that if there's ever any opera in Constantinople – the home of Orpheus* – Turkish ladies will be occupying the best box seats?"

"*Wives, you must submit to your own husbands*," Madame de Grancey kept muttering between clenched teeth. "This fellow Paul must have been a real brute."

"He was a bit of a hard man," replied the *abbé*, "and he insisted on taking charge of everything; he was patronizing towards St Peter, who was rather a nice man on the whole. And you mustn't take everything he said too literally. There are people who've blamed him for having a great weakness for Jansenism."

"Is that so?" hissed Madame de Grancey. "I had a suspicion that he was a heretic." And she went back to titivating herself.

# A Short Digression

WHEN THE QUINZE-VINGTS, the Institution for the Blind, was founded, we know that all were considered equal and everyone's little concerns were decided by vote at a general meeting. These blind people were perfectly capable of distinguishing, by touch, between gold and silver coins, not one of them would have mistaken wine from Brie for wine from Burgundy. Their sense of smell was more acute than that of people with two eyes. They could talk perfectly sensibly about matters pertaining to the four senses; that is to say that they knew everything about them that we're allowed to know. So they lived as peacefully and happily as you can expect if you happen to be blind. Unfortunately, one of their professors claimed to have clear ideas about eyesight: he persuaded people to listen to him, he schemed, he gathered an enthusiastic group of disciples and finally was acknowledged as the leader of the community. He started to lay down the law about colours. It was the beginning of the end.

This first dictator of the blind set up a small committee, thereby gaining control of all the alms they received, so that nobody would dare to resist him. He decreed that the clothes worn by the members of the Quinze-Vingts were white, and they believed him and would talk all the time about their lovely white coats, even though there wasn't a single white coat among the whole lot. Everyone else laughed at them, so they went and complained to the dictator. He told them that they were revolutionaries, malcontents, rebels allowing themselves to be led astray by the false ideas of people who had eyes and were daring to question the infallibility of their leader. This disagreement split the Quinze-Vingts into two factions.

To appease one of them, the dictator decreed that all their coats were red – there wasn't a single red coat in the whole Quinze-Vingts. They were laughed at even more. The community again complained. The dictator was furious and the other faction of the blind was furious too; this led to a long struggle and peace was restored only after all the Quinze-Vingts were granted permission to reserve judgement on the colour of their clothing.

A deaf man, on reading this little tale, admitted that the blind were wrong to make any statement about colours, but expressed his firm conviction that only the deaf had the right to pass judgement on music.

# An Adventure in India

## Translated by the Ignoramus

A S EVERYBODY KNOWS, during his stay in India, Pythagoras learnt the language of plants and animals from followers of that ancient Hindu sect, the gymnosophists, and, walking one day in a meadow not far from the sea, he heard a voice say:

"What a sad fate to have been born as grass! Barely have I been able to grow two inches tall before a devouring monster comes along, a horrible animal who tramples me under its big feet and whose jaws are armed with sharp fangs which it uses to cut me off and chew me up; then it swallows me. Men call this monster a sheep. I don't think that there's a more abominable creature in the whole wide world!"

Pythagoras continued his walk and, a few steps farther on, saw an oyster on a small rock. He wasn't yet following that admirable law which forbids us to eat animals, who are our fellow creatures, and was about to put the oyster in his mouth when it uttered this heart-rending cry:

"Oh, Nature! You created both grass and me – but grass is luckier! As soon as it's cut, it's reborn; it is immortal, but we poor oysters have no such advantage in our double armour-plated shell; we're eaten by the dozen by villainous people, at lunch, and that's the end of us for ever. What a dreadful fate to be born an oyster! How barbaric men are!"

Pythagoras shuddered. With tears in his eyes, realizing the enormity of the crime he was about to commit, he begged the oyster for forgiveness and placed it safely back on its rock.

As he was making his way back to the town, deep in meditation on this adventure, he saw some spiders eating flies, some swallows eating spiders and some sparrow hawks eating swallows. "None of those can be philosophers," he said to himself.

As he entered the town, he was jostled, pushed and knocked off his feet by a villainous-looking mob of men and women running along and shouting: "It's a good thing! It's a good thing! They deserve it!"

"What's a good thing? Who deserves what?" enquired Pythagoras, picking himself up.

The mob just kept on running, shouting: "How wonderful to see them being cooked!"

Pythagoras thought they must be referring to lentils or some other sort of vegetable. No, it wasn't that at all: it was two miserable Indians.

"Ah well, I suppose it'll be two great philosophers, tired of life and very happy to be reborn in another form. It's often a pleasure to change your abode, even though you're never really comfortable wherever you are. Anyway, there's no accounting for taste."

He made his way through the crowd and came to the public square where he saw a large pyre already alight, opposite which was a bench called a *tribunal*, with judges sitting on it. These judges were all holding a cow's tail in their hands and wearing on their heads a cap which looked exactly like the ears of the animal on which Silenus once came in bygone times, with Bacchus, after walking across the Red Sea without wetting his feet and having changed the course of both the sun and the moon, as faithfully recorded in the Orphic oracles.*

Among these judges there was a nice man whom Pythagoras knew; this Indian sage explained to the sage from Samos the nature of the entertainment that was about to be offered to the Hindu people.

"Those two Hindus," he said, "have no desire to be burnt alive. My worthy colleagues have condemned them to be tortured like this, one for having said that the substance of Xaca is not the same substance as Brahma and the other for suspecting that you could please the Supreme Being by virtuous acts without holding a cow's horn while you are dying, because, he says, you can't always be sure of having a cow's horn handy at that particular moment. The good women of the town were so frightened by both these heretical propositions that they gave the magistrates no peace until they ordered both these poor wretched creatures to be burnt at the stake."

Pythagoras thought to himself that there were many things to complain about, from grass to humans. But he succeeded in persuading the judges and even the bigoted females to see reason. This is the only time that this has ever happened.

Next, he went on to advocate tolerance to the inhabitants of Crotone, but an intolerant man set fire to his house and the man who had saved two Hindus from being burnt at the stake himself died in the flames.

It's every man for himself.

# The Adventure of Memory

T HAT PART OF MANKIND capable of thought – that is to say, one in a hundred thousand, at most – had long been hoping, or at least, kept on saying, that our ideas come to us through our senses and that memory is the only means by which we can join two thoughts or even two words together.

That is why Jupiter, the god of nature, fell in love with Mnemosyne, the goddess of memory, the moment he first set eyes on her, and their marriage gave birth to the nine Muses, who invented all the arts.

All our knowledge is based on this firm conviction and was universally accepted, even by the Nonsober,* when it was founded, even though it was true.

A short time later, an argumentative man, half geometrician, half fantasist,* came along and argued against the five senses and memory, and told the small minority of men capable of thought: "You've been misled until now. Your senses are useless, because ideas are innate and exist before your senses are capable of acting; you had all the necessary notions of time and space you require at birth. You had everything without having felt anything; all your ideas were born with you, they were part of your intelligence, which we call the soul. You had no need of memory; Memory's useless."

The Nonsober condemned that proposition, not because it was ridiculous but because it was new. However, when later on the Englishman Locke, in his *Essay Concerning Human Understanding*, had set about proving, extensively, that there were no innate ideas, that people had no greater need than what was provided by their five senses and that memory was very important indeed to retain what these senses have given us, the Nonsober condemned what it had previously considered true because it was being propounded by an Englishman. So it issued an order that in future mankind must believe in innate ideas and stop believing in our five senses and in memory. But instead of obeying the Nonsober, mankind laughed at it, which aroused such anger in the Nonsober that it wanted to have a philosopher burnt at the stake just because he'd pointed out that it was impossible to have a complete idea of cheese without ever seeing and eating some; this scoundrel had even dared to suggest that men or women would never have even woven tapestries if they'd not had needles and fingers to thread them with.

For the first time ever, the followers of Loyola supported the Nonsober and their deadly enemies, the followers of Jansen,* joined forces with them – momentarily. They called on the supreme judicial assembly of judges, very great hereditary philosophers – though shortly to be banned – to support them, and the judges outlawed memory, the five senses and the man who'd spoken up in favour of memory.

Present at this condemnation there happened to be a horse, he was not of the same species and there were various differences – size, voice, shagginess of hair – between him and mankind, but he had good sense and good senses, and one day he mentioned the matter to Pegasus, who was sharing his stables, and, with his customary volatility, Pegasus, that winged horse so favoured by the Muses, flew to them and told them what was happening.

For the last hundred years, the Muses had favoured that country where this scene had taken place and which had, before then, for a long time been barbarous. They were utterly scandalized by what Pegasus told them. They had great affection for their mother Memory or Mnemosyne, to whom they owed everything they knew, and were shocked by man's ingratitude. They didn't produce any satires against the former judges, the followers of Loyola and Jansen or the Nonsober, because satires never make anyone better: they merely irritate the stupid and make them even more unpleasant. They thought of a way to enlighten and at the same time punish them.

So it came about that one lovely night everyone's brain was so benumbed that when they woke up next morning every memory of the past had been obliterated. Acting from some instinct, not dependent on memory, some judges in bed with their wives tried to make closer contact with them. The wives, who very rarely have the instinct to embrace their husbands, sharply rejected their disgusting caresses. Their husbands were annoyed, the wives loudly protested and, in most households, they came to blows.

Gentlemen catching sight of a theologian's square hat used it to satisfy needs which can be relieved neither by memory nor by common sense. Ladies used pots standing on their dressing tables for similar purposes. Unable to remember their contracts with their masters, servants went into their bedrooms without realizing where they were; and man being a naturally curious animal, they opened all the drawers; and since man has a natural liking for the glitter of gold or silver (no memory is involved here), they took whatever came to hand. Their masters tried to cry "Stop, thief!" but the word "thief" having escaped their minds, it couldn't reach their tongue. They'd all forgotten the language they spoke, so they uttered meaningless grunts. It was far worse than the Tower of Babel, where everyone created a new language on the spot.

The innate fondness of men for pretty women was so strong that insolent young lackeys hurled themselves indiscriminately on the first woman or girl they met, whether she was an inn-keeper's wife or the wife of a high-court judge, and the women themselves, having forgotten everything they'd been told about modest behaviour, let them do whatever they wanted, without making any attempt to stop them.

It was time to eat: everybody had forgotten how to do it. Nobody had gone to market to buy or sell anything. Flunkeys had put on their masters' clothes and the masters were wearing those of their servants. They were all looking at each other completely bewildered. The people cleverest at providing themselves with what they needed – the common folk – found something to eat; the others went hungry.

The Lord Chief Justice and the Archbishop were walking around stark-naked and their grooms were wearing red silk gowns or priestly dalmatics. Everything was in confusion; starvation and disaster was threatening to exterminate everybody.

After a few days, the Muses took pity on this miserable race: they have good hearts, even if they do sometimes show their anger towards the wicked. They begged their mother to give back the memory she had taken away from them. Mnemosyne came down to the place where these contrary people dwelt and where they had insulted her in so foolhardy a manner. She addressed them in these words:

"Fools that you are, I forgive you. But once again remember that without the senses there can be no memory, and that without memory you are mindless."

The judges thanked her, rather ungraciously, and decided to issue a writ. The followers of Jansen published the story of this adventure in their gazette; it was clear that they had not yet learnt their lesson. The followers of Loyola started an intrigue at the Court on the subject. Coger* was completely at a loss and in his bewilderment, set his students this splendid subject for an essay: "*Non magis musis quam hominibus infensa est ista quæ vocatur memoria.*"*

# Notes

p. 13, *Phidias or Zeuxis*: Phidias and Zeuxis were respectively the foremost Greek sculptor and painter of the fifth century BC.

p. 14, *Demogorgon*: The eternal creator.

p. 18, *Pascal*: Blaise Pascal (1623–62) was a French mathematician, physicist and philosopher. He was so precociously gifted that he produced some of his most significant work in mathematics while still a teenager.

p. 20, *the illustrious vicar Derham*: William Derham (1657–1735) was an English theologian and scientist.

p. 20, *Lully*: Jean-Baptiste Lully (1632–87) was an Italian-born French court composer.

p. 26, *Father Castel*: Louis Bertrand Castel (1688–1757) was a French mathematician.

p. 32, *Leeuwenhoek and Hartsoeker... amazing*: Nicolaas Hartsoeker (1656–1725) and Antonie Philips van Leeuwenhoek (1632–1723), Dutch scientists who discovered spermatozoids from observing semen through a microscope.

p. 36, *Swammerdam... Réaumur*: Jan Swammerdam (1637–1680) was a Dutch biologist; René Antoine Ferchault de Réaumur (1683–1757) was a French scientist.

p. 40, *Malebranche... Locke's name was heard*: Nicolas Malebranche (1638–1715) was a French priest and philosopher who tried to reconcile the philosophical system of Decartes with that of religious thinkers such as St Augustine. Gottfried Wilhelm von Leibniz (1646–1716) was a German mathematician and philosopher who, among other things, was famous for his optimistic philosophy, which was much criticized by Voltaire. John Locke (1632–1704) was an English empiricist philosopher, famous for his theory of mind and often referred to as the father of classical liberalism.

p. 42, Thomas Aquinas (1225–74) was an Italian friar and scholastic philosopher. His theological magnum opus *Summa Theologica* is the most famous of his works.

p. 42, *the laughter of the gods*: A reference to *Iliad*, I, line 599, when the gods laugh at Hephaestus.

p. 65, *Jonah who was annoyed that they didn't destroy Nineveh*: In the Old Testament, Jonah is twice commanded by God to proclaim to the inhabitants of Nineveh that their city is doomed, but since they repent they are saved.

p. 75, *Zend-Avesta*: The principal scared text of Zoroastrianism.

p. 79, *Candia*: An ancient name for Crete.

p. 79, *I was descended... produced a monster*: According to Greek myth, Pasiphaë, the daughter of Helios, mated with a bull sent by Poseidon and gave birth to the Minotaur.

p. 80, *Maréchal d'Ancre... anyone who was interested*: Concino Concini (1575–1617), the Maréchal d'Ancre was a minister under Louis XIII of France who was allegedly assassinated under the orders of the young monarch.

p. 80, *the massacres of St Bartholomew*: The 1572 St Bartholomew's Day Massacre in Paris was a series of assassinations directed against the Huguenots during the French Wars of Religion.

p. 81, *Prime Minister Barnevelt*: A reference to Johan van Oldenbarnevelt (1547–1619), a Dutch statesman famous for his role in Holland's declaration of independence from Spain.

p. 87, *Aurangzeb*: Aurangzeb (1618–1707) was the sixth Mughal Emperor of the Indian subcontinent, who became a byword for wealth, power and military prowess.

p. 91, *the scaffold*: Charles I was executed in 1649; his wife, Henrietta Maria, was the youngest daughter of Henri IV of France.

p. 91, *eighteen years*: Mary, Queen of Scots was executed in 1587, after eighteen and a half years in custody.

p. 91, *Joanna of Naples*: The Queen was suffocated by Charles of Durazzo in 1382.

p. 92, *Niobe... Hecuba*: Mothers from classical mythology who were grief-stricken at the loss of their children.

p. 104, *Chlodio the Longhair*: Chlodio the Longhair was the Merovinginian King of the Franks from c.430 to c.450 AD.

p. 113, *wife of marshal of Grancey*: The second wife of the first Marshal of Grancey, Charlotte de Mornay, died in 1694.

p. 115, *Power belongs to him who can grow a beard*: The School for Wives (1662), Act III, Sc. 2.

p. 116, *Catherine*: Catherine the Great of Russia, who reigned from 1762 to 1796, and who famously corresponded with Voltaire.

p. 118, *Orpheus*: Legend has it that Orpheus came from the region of the Rhodope Mountains in southern Bulgaria.

p. 123, *Orphic oracles*: In fact, Voltaire has taken all these absurd details from a work, the *Demonstratio Evangelica* (1679), of the scholarly bishop Pierre Daniel Huet. Jokes about oracles being peddled to a gullible populace are as old as Aristophanes.

p. 125, *Nonsober*: Anagram of "Sorbonne".

p. 125, *half fantasist*: Descartes, the rationalist philosopher who believed in innate ideas.

p. 126, *followers of Jansen*: The Jansenists, who believed in predestination, as opposed to their bitter enemies the Jesuits, followers of Loyola, who taught that salvation could be earned.

p. 129, *Coger*: François-Marie Coger (1723–80), the rector of the Sorbonne at the time.

p. 129, *Non magis musis... quæ vocatur memoria*: "What is called memory is no more dangerous to the Muses than to men" (Latin).

# Acknowledgements

Professor Nicholas Cronk is grateful to The Leverhulme Trust for its award to the project *Constructing Contemporary History in the Enlightenment: Voltaire Historian.*